SLAUGHTER CITY

Its real name was Slautara, but the town was so wild and lawless they called it Slaughter City. No lawman had ever entered it and lived to tell the tale, but now former Marshal Greg McLure receives an order from the President of the United States; tame Slaughter City or die in the attempt. Driven and possessed as McLure is, he has no intention of dying – there are very strong reasons for hunting down the renegades of Slaughter City. Nevertheless his task is a formidable one and death will stalk him all the way.

SLAUGHTER CITY

SLAUGHTER CITY

by

Steve Musgrave

Dales Large Print Books
Long Preston, North Yorkshire,
BD23 4ND, England.

British Library Cataloguing in Publication Data.

Musgrave, Steve
    Slaughter City.

        A catalogue record of this book is
        available from the British Library

        ISBN   1-84262-262-5 pbk

First published in Great Britain in 2001 by Robert Hale Limited

Published in Large Print 2003 by arrangement with
Robert Hale Ltd.

Dales Large Print is an imprint of Library Magna Books Ltd.

Printed and bound in Great Britain by
T.J. (International) Ltd., Cornwall, PL28 8RW

X000 000 031 2160

ONE

The detachment of cavalry was drawn up in order, fifty strong, on the plain in the dusk. It was a cold Texas evening in November, but Major Jennings had refused to allow his men to wear their overcoats. These were still folded in front of their heavy McClellan saddles. The major believed that there was killing to be done that evening and he was of the opinion that troopers fought best unencumbered.

Lieutenant Wayland galloped back across the plain from his scouting mission and drew up his horse hard next to his superior officer's. His smooth cheeks were flushed with excitement and anticipation and his eyes sparkled as brightly as the solitary gold bar on his shoulder. Wayland was twenty, ambitious, enthusiastic and permanently disappointed because the war was drawing to a close and so far he had played little part in it.

'Report,' growled Major Jennings.

'Hell, Major, what's to report?' demanded Wayland petulantly, gesturing behind him. 'There's nothing but a mile of open country before we get to the mesa. You can see that for yourself.'

Jennings screwed up his eyes. Warily through the gloom he surveyed the intervening distance between his troop and the lights of the small town just visible beyond the ridge cutting through the flat-topped cliff.

'There must be something,' he said, chewing worriedly on the frayed ends of his drooping, overgrown moustache. 'They wouldn't just let us ride in on 'em, like it was a come-to-prayer meeting.'

'That's just what they have done!' burst out the lieutenant impatiently, unable to restrain himself. 'After all, what are they but a bunch of deserters and outlaws?'

'They're men who've fought on both sides at Bull Run, Shiloh and Gettysburg, that's who,' snapped the major. 'There ain't a thing about war and fighting they ain't seen and done.'

'They're cowards and traitors,' returned the young lieutenant scornfully. 'Believe me, Major, Slautara's there for the taking. Let's ride in and get ourselves some glory!'

A weary half-smile creased the major's thin face like a knifecut. 'There won't be no glory on offer tonight,' he responded with quiet conviction. 'The glory days are long-gone. What's left is scavenging. Just plain ornery scavenging.'

Decisively he turned his horse away from the lieutenant's and pretended to inspect his company for one last time, while he tried to work matters out in his mind. Automatically his eyes took in the accoutrements of the troopers lined up before him on their mounts. Apart from a couple of good poker players and expert thieves who had secured coveted buckskin jackets for themselves, the soldiers all wore the basic dark-blue blouses and light blue pants with the yellow stripes of the Union cavalryman down the legs. Most wore leather knee boots. Each man had a single-shot Springfield carbine in a long holster at his side.

There the similarities ended. These were experienced soldiers and over the four long years of the Civil War each veteran had carefully accumulated his own store of additional clothing to guard against the rigours of the elements on active service. Some had fashioned rough cloaks out of the blue and orange Army-issue saddle blankets and wore them draped over their shoulders. Others had two sets of long-johns beneath their uniforms, giving them the swollen and distended appearance of over-stuffed scarecrows. A few wore 'coon-skin caps instead of the regulation peaked headwear. Most of the troopers were unshaven.

None of this worried Jennings. He knew that these were tough, experienced fighting men who would follow him stolidly wherever he cared to lead. He only hoped that he was about to take them in the right direction. No matter how hard he tried he could not shake off a sense of grim foreboding that something dreadful was about to happen that night.

'All right,' he said grimly. 'Let's get this damn thing over with.'

He sat slumped, fretting in his saddle, as Lieutenant Wayland started barking unnecessary orders in an attempt to worry the troops into the half-moon formation they would have adopted by themselves with ease. Finally, a sweating Wayland spurred his horse over to the major.

'All ready, sir,' he announced triumphantly.

Jennings nodded and returned the other officer's salute in a perfunctory manner. He stood in his stirrups and half raised an arm.

'For-ward!' he shouted.

The horsemen began to knee their mounts forward in a trot across the dark plain toward the distant lights of the town beyond the pass. They moved steadily, without undue haste but with no laggards either, maintaining a regular, pulsating line.

'What did I tell you, Major?' shouted Lieutenant Wayland excitedly, galloping up to Jennings and riding next to him. 'They ain't caught sight of hide nor hair of us.'

'Take your place in line, Mr Wayland,' ordered the major tersely.

The lieutenant turned red and dropped back. Jennings twisted in his saddle to give the order to extend the trot to a canter. Before he could open his mouth the earth erupted beneath the hoofs of his horse.

There was a mighty roar. The earth seemed to rise around them in a great flame-flecked cloud. It took with it rocks, men and horses in a frightening arc. Debris flew through the air amid a shower of smoke and dust. The screams of dead and injured men mingled to form an ear-splitting cacophony.

When the dust and smoke started to drift away there was a crater in the plain twenty feet deep and sixty feet round. The hole was filled with soldiers and their mounts, some struggling feebly through the freshly loosened blocks of clay, but the majority still and rigid in the dreadful discipline of death.

Bleeding from half-a-dozen wounds and with one ear-drum shattered, Lieutenant Wayland struggled dazedly across the crater to the side of his commanding officer. Major Jennings was lying on his back. One of his arms had been torn off at the shoulder, and what were left of his legs were trapped beneath a raft of crumpled pit props. His eyes flickered open and he recognized the lieutenant.

'The bastards dug a mine and filled the shaft with powder,' he said faintly. 'When they saw us hurrahing across the plain they lit the fuses. We rode straight into their trap.'

With a sob Wayland started to use his torn and bleeding hands to dig desperately in an effort to free his company commander. Jennings stopped him with a faint movement of his remaining hand.

'I'm done for,' he said faintly, grimacing with pain. 'Maybe I'm the lucky one at that.

Won't matter none to me when they call it Jennings' Folly. Gather together the survivors and get them out of this damned grave.'

'Am I to carry on the attack, sir?' asked Wayland, swaying confusedly.

A bitter laugh escaped from the dying man's lips. It changed almost at once to an agonized cough.

'Hell no!' he croaked. 'Won't be more than ten whole men left alive after this. Save yourselves. The army's never going to take Slautara.'

Wayland nodded bemusedly and half turned away. He heard the major speak again and limped back to him, straining to hear. 'I told you there would be no glory on this mission,' said Jennings through rigid lips in a voice that was little more than a sigh. 'The army will do its best to save its face and hush this one up, boy. Take my word for it. You've just ridden in a phantom attack!'

TWO

McLure had been waiting all morning for the chance to steal the neglected tin cup half-full of water from the guards. He was sitting on the sun-baked earth of the compound on the outer edge of one of the many restless groups of Confederate prisoners inside the towering stone walls of Hartson prison.

Armed Union guards were stationed every twenty yards along the top of the flat raised walkway just behind the palisade. Over the reinforced-iron main gates two uniformed corporals manned a 12-pound howitzer trained on the compound. Other guards walked round the edges of the massed prisoners or stood idly chatting in twos and threes. There were over a thousand of the toughest and most escape-prone Confederate prisoners-of-war in Hartson, rebellious malcontents concentrated in the one prison, where equally brutal guards could attempt to contain them by force and starvation.

McLure sat immobile, his tall emaciated frame looking as if it was carved out of weathered granite. He had lost forty pounds in weight since he had been taken at Shiloh, but still there was not a man in Hartson who would dare approach him uninvited.

One of the bored guards he was watching turned away to spit. As he did so he masked the view of the second sentry. It was the instant McLure had been waiting for. His long arm snaked out and grasped the tin cup. In the same movement he rolled over back into the main group and stood up, without spilling a drop of the precious liquid. He shouldered his way through the morose, shuffling prisoners and was soon lost to sight amid the shifting sea of tattered blue-and-grey uniforms.

He headed for the hospital behind the

rows of tattered tents housing the prisoners. It was a makeshift building erected by the Confederates themselves from a few timber supports and a number of horizontal slats which served poorly to keep out the rain. Rows of groaning men lined the sides. Near the entrance half-a-dozen occupied stretchers were aligned, ready to be carried outside. These were the patients either already dead or deemed to be close to death. An outbreak of typhoid had carried off a hundred prisoners in the last week alone. This accounted for the lack of orderlies in the hospital. No Union private was going to risk his life for the sake of a bunch of Johnny Rebs, with the war all but won and lost anyway.

McLure made his way to one of the stretchers by the door. The man lying on the wooden framework was almost as tall as he was, but ten years older. The eyes of the dying man flickered open. He tried to twist his face into a welcoming grin.

'Hi, Cap'n,' he whispered painfully. 'No

call for you to come here. Appreciate it, though.'

'Take it easy, Sergeant-Major,' said McLure. 'I've brought you some water.'

The sergeant-major's eyes widened. 'How in hell did you manage that?' he asked incredulously. 'They ain't given us spit to drink for twenty-four hours.'

'Present from some Union boys,' said McLure. He cradled his arm under the other man's head and raised it so that some of the water could trickle past his parched and cracked lips. The sergeant-major drank deeply until the cup was empty. Tenderly McLure let the older man's head sink back on to the stretcher.

'I was going to say you've saved my life,' said the sergeant-major with an effort. 'Reckon that would be overstating it a mite though.'

'You'll pull through this just like you've pulled through everything else,' said McLure with a conviction he was not feeling. 'You're too ornery to die, Tom Skellett.'

The sergeant-major shook his head. 'Not this time,' he said feebly. 'Reckon they put me at one fence too many. Still, we gave them a run for their money.' His eyes glinted. 'But there wasn't no need for any of it. If our flank had held at Vicksburg we could still have fought our way out. If Major Glanville hadn't taken his company out of the line we would have won that battle.'

'Maybe,' said McLure expressionlessly.

'Now there's only you and me left, Cap'n McLure. Two out of the seventy-five they took at Shiloh. Pretty soon there's going to be only you.'

McLure opened his mouth to protest but the other man reached out and grabbed his hand fiercely. 'Hear me out, Greg,' he said. 'You're ace-high with me. You survive this hell-hole, do you hear? You get out in one piece. And when you do, find that scum Glanville and kill him like a dog. Promise me that.'

'I promise,' said McLure laconically. 'I'd 'a done it anyhow.'

Skellett's eyes searched the officer's intently. Then he nodded, as if satisfied with what he saw.

'Reckon I can die content now,' he said flatly, and turned his face to the wall. The troubles and hardships of a lifetime's soldiering eased out of his face, to leave it suddenly smooth and calm.

McLure squatted by the dead man's side for a few minutes, his head bowed. Then he stood up and started to put his plan into action. Gathering what remained of his strength he lifted Skellett's body from the stretcher and carried it over to the side of the ward, placing it by the side of one of the sick men. If any of the patients noticed what he was doing none had enough strength or interest to protest. Then McLure walked back to the stretcher and took the dead sergeant-major's place on it.

He had to wait several hours before two medical orderlies with bandages fixed in place over their noses and mouths as makeshift masks came in reluctantly and started carrying out the dead. McLure had to lie there another thirty minutes until it was his turn. He closed his eyes as he felt his stretcher being lifted. Soon he was conscious of being carried across the compound towards the main gate. The corpses would be tossed into a pit and burnt with quicklime a mile out into the desert. Somehow or other he would either escape or be gunned down before they got him as far as the corrosive trench.

'Stop!' cracked an order across the compound. 'Put that stretcher down at once.'

McLure stifled a curse and squinted out through half-closed eyes as his stretcher was deposited roughly on the ground. He was still fifty yards from the gates. Captain Jerome, the camp's medical officer, was peering down suspiciously at him. Jerome was a fat, indolent man in his late twenties, sweating although it was a cold February day.

'That's McLure, you fools!' he said accusingly to the orderlies. 'McLure wasn't sick in the hospital.'

As he spoke, the doctor knelt by the side of the stretcher and felt McLure's pulse. He glared up at the stretcher bearers.

'It's stronger than mine,' he whined. 'He's trying to escape again, and you fools were going to carry him out of the camp!'

McLure opened his eyes resignedly and stood up. He was aware of the other prisoners looking on appreciatively, and of the guards on the wall, suddenly alert, their rifles pointing at him.

'Nothing personal,' he said. 'Only I reckoned I was going to take sick, so I thought I'd save time and jump straight into the lime-pit before I let you put your slimy hands on me.'

There was a roar of laughter from those Confederates close enough to hear him. Captain Jerome turned scarlet. He shouted to one of the guards close at hand. The man shouldered his way through the throng and smashed the stock of his carbine into McLure's ribs. The Confederate officer retched and sank to his knees. He forced himself to stand erect and stood glaring at Jerome. The fat doctor smirked.

'You're still too healthy to pass as a sick man,' he jeered. 'A word of advice, McLure. If you ever want to convince people that you're close to dying, get a fever, man. If you've got a fever you can convince people you've got just about anything.'

'Is that a fact,' grunted McLure. 'Well, here's another instant, correct diagnosis for you. You're a fat pig's arse.'

Jerome took a furious step forward. Something in the steel of McLure's gaze made the medical officer restrain himself. Petulantly he turned to the guard. 'Take him to the sweat-hole,' he commanded, trembling with rage. 'Let's see if the captain enjoys playing his games there.'

Some of the other prisoners, reinvigorated by McLure's escape bid, began to protest. Three other guards forced their way through the crowd and began to hustle McLure away. The sentries on the walkway trained their rifles on the compound. Someone shouted an order and more Union troops came running out of the wooden barracks.

Reluctantly the mutinous mob of prisoners scattered. A harassed-looking young lieutenant suddenly appeared in the doorway of the wooden administration building and beckoned the guards to bring McLure over to him.

'All right,' he said impatiently as the soldiers delivered their charge. 'Forget the sweat-hole for the time being. The camp commandant wants to see him. I'll take over. You three wait outside.'

The lieutenant conducted the puzzled but impassive McLure inside the building and past the corporal clerk sitting in the outer office. He knocked on the door of the commandant's room and ushered McLure in, withdrawing at once.

There were two men sitting inside the sparsely furnished office. The short, lean figure of Colonel Novak, the commandant, was standing at the window, scowling out

24

over the compound, as neat as a tailor's dummy. Sitting slumped in front of the desk was a burly, middle-aged civilian, a few years over forty, in a shapeless grey suit. He was chomping on a cigar. A full beard burst excitedly from his cheeks and fell to his chest, like poor-quality cotton escaping from a pod. His tired, cynical eyes settled on McLure and did not look away again for the duration of their encounter.

Colonel Novak adjusted his sword in its scabbard and walked back and sat behind his desk. He always looked more like a strutting actor playing an officer than the real thing, thought McLure.

'This is McLure,' Novak said, as if the very admission hurt him.

The bearded man nodded slightly 'Mc-Lure,' he said, in a pleasant Scottish rumble, 'I've got a job for you, laddie.'

'I don't work for the Union,' said McLure uncompromisingly.

'I told you so,' said Novak triumphantly. 'He's a trouble-maker. He's made four escape attempts in the last fifteen months.'

'Five,' said McLure, 'but who's counting?'

The bearded man ignored the exchange, like a benevolent schoolteacher with squabbling students.

'I'm not asking you to work for the Union, son,' he said mildly. 'I'm asking you to work for your country.'

'I don't have a country,' said McLure. 'Not no more.'

'There,' said Novak vindictively. 'What did I tell you? You're wasting your time.'

The bearded man stood up. He looked grave. 'You have a country, Captain McLure,' he told the other man. 'A divided country, that's for sure, and one in sore need of healing, but one country for all that. I can tell you, sir, that this War Between the States will end within the next three months, with the surrender of the Southern forces. And that is why President Lincoln needs your help, sir.'

'What makes you so sure the war will end?' asked McLure.

He tried to sound contemptuous but he

knew in his heart that the other man was probably right. The last batch of prisoners to be brought in had reported that most of the major Southern cities had been reduced to ruins and the countryside stripped bare of food and stock.

'This here is Mr Allan Pinkerton,' said Colonel Novak bombastically. 'Head of the Union intelligence services and personal friend to Abe Lincoln himself.'

McLure surveyed Pinkerton with sudden interest. The bearded man continued to return his gaze unblinkingly.

'I've heard of you,' acknowledged McLure. 'They say you're more use to the Union than a regiment of troops.'

'Then they exaggerate,' said Pinkerton. 'But you, Captain McLure, can be of the greatest service, if you undertake the commission I bring you from the president.'

'You must be mad if you think I'd lift a finger to help the men I fought for two years,' said McLure bitterly.

'Just hear me out,' said Pinkerton steadily.

'Have you ever heard of Slaughter City?'

'No.'

'Not many have – yet. It's a town called Slautara in Texas. For years it was just another no-account cow-town stuck among the mountains, but for the past year it's been growing like a weed, because deserters from both sides have been flocking there and turning it into an armed garrison. Added to that, every outlaw on the run in the West seems to have holed up there. It's a wide-open place. It's not the sort of town that the president wants to have around while he's trying to rebuild the country.'

'Then send in the troops,' said McLure brusquely. 'Even a Union force ought to be able to take a place like that.'

'It's been tried,' said Pinkerton tersely. 'Three months ago, a reinforced company of cavalry were sent in to raze the place. The inhabitants of the town dug an earthworks on the plain outside, and blew the advancing company to kingdom-come. There were twelve survivors. You see, Captain McLure,

Slaughter City isn't just a rabble: it's a highly organized fortress under the command of somebody who knows what he's doing. There's no way the Union commanders are going to risk another force on a frontal attack. If it failed, the publicity would be deadly.'

'Then send in undercover agents,' said McLure.

'We have. Three of my best men have tried to infiltrate the town. Their bodies all turned up on the plain outside Slaughter City. That's why we want you to go in.'

'Me?' asked McLure, almost unable to believe what he had heard. 'What the hell makes you think I'd risk my life on a crazy mission like that?'

'I told you the town was being run by someone special, a man tough enough and bright enough to unite Union and Confederate deserters and the outlaws in the place.' Pinkerton paused. 'We now know who that man is. It's Major John Glanville.'

'Glanville?' echoed McLure dully, feeling

29

as if he had been struck a physical blow.

Pinkerton nodded. 'The one who turned and ran at Shiloh, exposing your flank and leading to the death of over a hundred men in your company, and the rest of you being taken prisoner and spending the last two years here. That's why I've come today.' He indicated the commandant. 'Colonel Novak's guards keep their eyes and ears open. They know how much you and your men hated Glanville for what he did. The colonel tells me that there are now only two survivors of the massacre–'

'I'm the only one left,' interrupted McLure.

'Skellett's gone, has he?' said Novak callously. 'That would probably account for the ruckus you were making out in the compound just now.'

'Just you remaining,' repeated Pinkerton. 'That means you're the only one who can get to Glanville. You've never seen each other, have you? Glanville joined your 5th Virginians late in the campaign.'

'Never,' said McLure. 'What makes you think I can do it?'

'I don't,' said Pinkerton coolly. 'You probably can't. But you've got a better chance than most. You were a hero at Shiloh. Before the war you were a lawman. The colonel tells me that you're the toughest and meanest bastard in this camp. You hate Glanville. Put all those together and you might just have a prayer.'

'And if you don't,' gloated Novak with a quiet, venomous satisfaction, 'it won't matter a damn.'

'If I do get to Glanville I'll kill him,' warned McLure.

'I wouldn't have it any other way,' shrugged Pinkerton. 'I want Glanville dead and Slaughter City destroyed.'

Novak stood up. 'You'll be leaving with Mr Pinkerton in an hour,' he said briskly. 'He wants to spend a couple of months feeding you up and getting you back into shape.'

'You knew I was going to agree, didn't

you?' McLure asked him.

A rare cold smile touched the sides of the colonel's mouth. 'Sure I knew,' he agreed. 'You've fought on the losing side in the war and your company was cut to ribbons around you. You're aiming all your hate directly at Glanville, which suits the Union just fine. Go and look for Glanville, McLure. You've got nowhere else to go!'

THREE

They had been riding for three days, stopping only to snatch time to eat and sleep along the trail. They had said little. Most of what was necessary had been talked through on the ranch to which Pinkerton had taken McLure when they had left the prison camp eight weeks before.

They had spent much of each day for the eight weeks on the open range, far from the bunkhouse, returning only at night to eat. The time had been spent in toughening McLure up and honing his neglected skills with the Colt and the Winchester. At first, after his long sojourn in the prison camp, he had been weak and awkward, but good food and long days in the saddle had hardened him to a peak again. He even put on twenty pounds of muscle and sinew during his brief time on the range. His abilities with a revolver and rifle came back as if they had never left him.

Once, in the early hours of the morning, he had woken up to find Pinkerton sitting by the cold stove in the bunkhouse, staring reflectively at him.

'Making sure I don't escape?' McLure had asked sourly.

'Thought never entered my mind,' Pinkerton had answered. 'You won't find a Confederate force to escape to. Jeff Davies reckons two-thirds of his army has deserted. I give the war another month. Go and look for it if you like.'

'I've had my share of war,' McLure had growled in reply. 'Killing Glanville will be enough for me.'

'Laddie,' said Pinkerton contentedly, 'you've got enough pure spite inside you to start your own private war.'

They had never broached the subject again. At the end of the two-month period they had caught an overland stage to Fort

Worth, where horses and supplies had been waiting for them. Then they had headed straight for Slautara, stopping only when they had reached this rocky outcrop on the outskirts of the plain leading to the mesa sheltering the town.

'Slaughter City is about five miles ahead,' said Pinkerton. 'Good luck!'

'Did you get me what I asked for?' McLure demanded.

'Almost forgot,' apologized Pinkerton. The Scot dismounted and took a small twist of paper from his saddle-bag. He handed it to McLure, who tucked it into a pocket.

'Had to get it special from a mining camp,' he grumbled. 'Be careful how you handle it. There isn't much there, but it's terrible dangerous.'

'Ain't hardly going into a job that's safe,' said McLure.

'You're right there,' said Pinkerton, turning his horse. 'Try to get word to me of what you're doing. I'm going to leave one of my men here. His name's Kelly. Red-haired fellow. Ride out when you can and meet him here. He'll pass anything on to me.'

'I'll do my best,' said McLure.

Pinkerton extended a large hand. '*Adios, McLure.*'

McLure shook the other man's hand without comment. He booted his horse away across the plain in the direction of the mesa. Before he had gone more than a few yards he had almost forgotten the Union spy-master. McLure was under no illusions about the purpose of his mission. Pinkerton was using him as a human grenade, to be hurled into the town and left there either to explode or be extinguished. If he killed Glanville it would help the authorities. If Glanville got to him first he would be just another no-account dead Confederate soldier among thousands of others. None of that mattered. He would willingly give up his own life if it meant killing the man who had been responsible for the deaths of the men in McLure's company.

While he was still some way from the town

he stopped and dismounted behind a clump of aspen trees. From his saddle-bag he took a small square of muslin. He had bought a length of the cloth at a store during their stop-over in Forth Worth. Working laboriously at night, away from the prying eyes of Pinkerton, he had sewn the muslin into a pocket with an opening on one side. Now he took the twist of paper from his pocket and emptied its contents into the square, securing the mouth with a length of twine. He stripped off his shirt and tucked the packet inside a length of leather strapping he had already wound across his chest. Then he took off one of his boots and placed three matches in it before replacing it. He was still wearing the tattered remnants of his Confederate uniform, freshly patched and darned. He shrugged back into his shirt and remounted.

He reached the mesa shortly before noon. The rocky walls climbed high into the sky. An aperture about a hundred yards wide led through the cliffs to the town beyond. A river snaked along its length. Anyone approaching Slautara would have to ride through the narrow canyon or try to scale the heights of the mesa, no easy task. The cliffs extended for miles on both sides of the canyon and then curved round to surround the town. The place was a natural bolt-hole. He noticed the complete absence of telegraph wires. It looked as if news into and out of the town was strictly controlled.

McLure reined in his horse and waited. He had seen the two armed guards perched on top of a pile of rocks some time ago as he had cantered across the plain. Both men were clad in work-shirts and Levis. They carried repeating rifles in their hands and looked mean.

'Who are you and what do you want?' shouted one of them.

'Name's McLure,' he answered calmly. Pinkerton had insisted on his keeping as close to the truth as possible whenever he should be interrogated. That way there would be fewer chances to trip him up.

'Why have you come here?'

'I could handle a little shelter for a week or two.'

The guard who was doing the talking nodded. Plainly he had heard this response before.

'Shelter don't come cheap,' he replied automatically.

'I can pay my way.'

The guard nodded unemotionally and fired his rifle once in the air as a signal to those waiting in the town. He gestured to McLure to ride on. The tall man nodded and booted his horse forward.

He followed the trail of the river through the canyon. The town spreading wide at the far end of the valley came as a surprise to him. He had been expecting a mean huddle of shacks, but this was a respectable, medium-sized town nestling in the shade of the mesa, with the river curling round its edges. The main street was broad and busy, with wagons and traps rattling busily along its length. For a small town it was liberally supplied with stores, diners and saloons, all doing good business so early in the afternoon. He could even see a sheriff's office.

Three men were waiting for him on the outskirts of the settlement. All three were in faded Confederate uniforms. Two of them wore sergeants' stripes, while the third carried the insignia of a captain. It was the officer who spoke. He was a slim, good-looking man with the easy affability of a snake-oil salesman.

'Hi,' he said pleasantly, with a smile that came a little too readily. 'Welcome to Slaughter City. Come along to the sheriff's office and we'll get the formalities over. My name's Pete Duvall.'

Duvall led the way along the street towards the office. The two sergeants flanked McLure watchfully. No one else in the street seemed to be paying much attention to the group. McLure descended from his horse and tied the reins to a hitching rail by the boardwalk. He followed the captain into the office. One of the sergeants came in at his heels. The second non-com stopped to remove the saddle-bags from McLure's mount and brought them into the office, kicking the door shut behind him.

'Well now,' said Duvall, dropping into the chair behind the desk. 'Suppose you tell me what brings you here.'

'My name's McLure,' said the big man, trying to sound reluctant. 'I was told I could hole up here for a while.'

'Well, you were told right,' said Duvall. 'Let's see if you can afford to pay your board.'

He signalled to the sergeant with the saddlebags. The man emptied their contents on to the table. Several wads of notes and a few pieces of jewellery spilled over the surface. The sergeant counted the notes quickly.

'Four hundred dollars and some bits and pieces worth maybe another hundred or so,' he growled.

Duvall raised an eyebrow. 'Not bad,' he

drawled. 'We get some saddle-tramps passing through who come in with less than a hundred in their poke. I ask you, where do they think they are? We'll take two hundred and fifty and that diamond ring. The rest you can keep.'

'The hell you will,' growled McLure.

'Take a look behind you,' invited Duvall.

McLure turned. The first sergeant had drawn his service revolver and had levelled it at him. The other non-com swiftly counted out $250 and threw the notes on to the desk, together with the diamond ring. Deftly, Duvall creamed a few notes off the top of the wad, selected two rings from the pile and put them all into a drawer.

'This buys you ten days in Slautara,' he said. 'After that you either ride on, or you come up with another two hundred and fifty.'

'Town tax,' added the second sergeant with a guffaw.

'Looks like you got this place locked up tight,' McLure commented grimly, pocketing what was left of his bankroll.

'We like to think so,' said the officer. 'We'll take your gun as well. It'll be returned to you when you move on, or if you ride out on a job.'

'Which ought to be pretty soon,' sneered the first sergeant. 'The money you got left won't buy you much in this place.'

'Where did you get your poke?' asked Duvall idly.

'Stage-coach outside San Angelo,' said McLure.

It was true. Pinkerton had given him the money and the information. The outlaw concerned had been caught and hanged a week ago, with most of his take intact.

'Where did you come from before that?' asked the second sergeant.

'Army,' said McLure shortly. 'Fourth Kentucky Cavalry,' he added, lying smoothly. The Kentucky had been stationed a long way from the Virginians at Shiloh.

'Rode away from the guns, eh?' asked Duvall. 'A lot of us had the sense to do that.' He paused and then added casually, 'You

43

got any specialities – explosives, signals, that sort of thing?'

McLure shook his head. 'I can ride and shoot, is all,' he replied.

The officer lost interest transparently. He stood up abruptly, shovelling the remainder of the money and jewellery back at the other man.

'Just one town law,' said Duvall. 'Don't make trouble. There are a lot of what you might call sensitive men in this town. All they want is a little peace and quiet. We aim to give it to 'em – at a price. Step out of line and we'll kill you.'

'You running this operation?' McLure asked.

'None of your damned business,' said Duvall curtly. 'You've bought and paid for ten days. Now hand over your gun-belt and get out.'

McLure left the sheriff's office with the mocking laughter of the sergeants ringing in his ears. It was a sweet operation, he conceded as he walked his horse down the street towards the livery stables. The men running the town were using it as a bunk-house for outlaws who could afford to pay rent money between jobs. What was more, they were being encouraged to spend the money they had left in the saloons and dancehalls. Presumably Glanville took a cut from these as well. Far from being the wide-open town he had expected, Slautara was being led on a tight rein.

He reached the livery stable and handed over his mount to a hulking farrier in a sweat-stained undershirt.

'Feed and water him,' he ordered.

'That'll be two dollars a day,' growled the farrier.

'How much?' complained McLure. 'I didn't pay that much for a hotel room in San Francisco.'

'This ain't San Francisco,' replied the blacksmith with an evil grin. 'This is Slaughter City. In advance, mister.'

Reluctantly McLure handed over ten dollars and headed for the saloon. There were many more men than women in the street, but the town had a prosperous air to it. The only men wearing guns were a sprinkling of soldiers in Confederate uniforms, presumably providing back-up for Duvall and the others. They eased their way watchfully through the crowds, accorded plenty of room and respect by the others.

McLure moved carefully through the crowds on the boardwalk. The last time he had seen a town as outwardly prosperous as this had been Virginia City in 1860, just after the Comstock gold lode had been struck at the Washoe Diggings, sparking off the great Nevada rush. McLure suppressed a surge of rage at the sight of the well-fed ordinary citizens of the town flocking along the shopping strip. While the rest of Texas starved under the boots of the invading Union army, these respectable men and women were benefiting from Slaughter City's prosperity just as much as the outlaws.

Ahead of him he could see the largest saloon. Automatically he flexed and unflexed his shoulders. He had not reckoned on being deprived of his pistol, but if he was going to attract the attention of Glanville quickly there was only one way of doing so that he could think of.

McLure shouldered his way in through the batwing doors of the saloon. The place was crowded, with men jostling three-deep at the long bar. Three harrassed bar-dogs in soiled aprons were struggling to cope with the orders across the counter awash with spilled liquor. No one paid any attention to him as he came in and stood by the doors. There was no doubt about it, Slautara was a prosperous town.

It took him several minutes to shoulder his way through to the bar and order a beer. A number of men scowled at him as he edged past them, but none cared to take issue with the broad-shouldered, hard-faced stranger with the cold eyes. McLure shovelled across the seventy cents demanded for a two-bit glass and took his beer to an empty chair at a table.

An old-timer in a tattered buckskin shirt and stained Levis was already sitting at the table. His wispy white hair hung like tattered streamers to his shoulders. He looked as if he had been nursing his beer for a long time.

'Howdy,' he said hopefully, as McLure joined him. 'New to Slautara?'

McLure nodded and stared round the room, taking in the piano player in the corner working unsteadily through 'Sweet Evelina', the busy faro table, the hostesses plying their trade with the booze-blind drunks, and the observant, swivel-eyed houseman sitting on a raised wooden chair against one wall, with a scattergun cradled on his lap.

'Been here long?' he asked the old man.

'A week,' replied his companion bitterly. 'All I could afford. Got to move out tomorrow. Are you going to buy me a drink?'

'Maybe,' said McLure, his eyes still searching the bar.

'What you looking for?' asked the old man.

'Who,' asked McLure deliberately, 'would you say was the toughest guy in this room?'

The other man leant back in his chair. 'Depends what you mean by tough,' he said judiciously. 'Lot of those guys think they're hard badmen from Bitter Creek. Some of 'em are. Do you mean best to burn powder, fastest with a knife, or just plain loco? Bat Hennery over there sewed up his own side from armpit to waist with a needle and thread after it had been laid open by a bear up in the mountain country, if that's what you're looking for.'

'Best with his fists,' said McLure.

'That's a horse of a different colour,' said the old man. Unhesitatingly he indicated a massive man with a pot belly drinking noisily with a group of others at the bar. 'Luke Connolly,' he said. 'Never seen him bested yet. Hell, never even seen anyone bother to take him on lately.'

'Connolly, huh?' said McLure sliding a dollar across the table top. 'Which hand does he favour?'

'His left is like an artillery piece.'

'Thanks,' said McLure, standing up.

'Mind you,' said the old man equably, 'his right is like a rockslide.'

'Great help,' said McLure drily. 'Go and buy your beer.'

'If you're a-going to do what I think you're a-going to do,' said the old man, settling back into his seat with cackling relish, 'reckon I'll stay right here and enjoy the fight while it lasts. You won't be over there long enough for my thirst to increase much. Five gets you twenty they carry you out on a timber.'

'You ain't got five,' said McLure. He pushed his way back through the throng towards Connolly. Close-up from behind, the man looked enormous, a good six and a half feet tall and as broad as a barn-door. His hair hung down to his shoulders and he had not shaved for a week. McLure wished that he could have had another month's recuperation on Pinkerton's ranch. He tapped Connolly on the shoulder. Slowly the giant turned to face him. Conversation in the vicinity died away.

'What the hell do you want?' he growled, glowering at McLure, his glass of raw white whisky almost lost from sight in his massive hand.

McLure pulled back his left and drove it with all his might into Connolly's un-protected face. The pain of the blow shot up his arm clear through to the shoulder. Connolly's knees buckled slightly and he let out a roar of fury. Then he lurched forward blindly at his assailant, while the sur-rounding drinkers scattered in all directions.

McLure shuffled backwards, his arms held high and his eyes watching the big man's feet to see how Connolly was setting himself for his punches. The big man blundered after him, almost falling in his haste to reach his tormentor. McLure snaked out his left twice, closing one of the giant's eyes. Connolly roared again and swung all his weight behind an over-arm right. McLure moved inside the arc and beat a vicious tattoo of punches against the other man's ribs. Connolly tried to grab him in a bearhug but McLure had moved out of range again and was circling him lightly, moving backwards and forwards with threatening movements.

Everyone in the saloon was on his feet and cheering on the contestants, giving them just enough room in which to fight. Out of the corner of his eye McLure could see the houseman uncertainly on his feet, shifting his scattergun from hand to hand. Desperately he hoped that the gunman would regard the fight in the light of bar entertainment and would not let fly with a load of buckshot in an effort to clear the floor.

Connolly's chest was heaving as he lumbered relentlessly after his adversary. Again he swung his wide right, as if he was throwing a stone for distance. Once more McLure moved inside and hooked his left twice into the big man's kidneys. He heard Connolly groan. McLure moved back and then stopped and cracked his left into Connolly's nose. It exploded in a thick spray of blood. The excited onlookers bayed at the sight of the gushing red fountain.

McLure kept circling, avoiding the other man's ponderous rushes. Connolly was strictly a strong man, he decided. What he knew about fighting he could have carved on the head of a nickel. He had achieved his reputation through his size and strength. Perhaps he was also durable, but McLure hoped not.

He moved in on the big man, hooking and jabbing with his left and following the punches with an occasional stiff right cross, all aimed at the giant's face and throat. He tried to avoid shattering his hands on the other man's skull, and kept his elbows pulled in tight to his ribs, so that he could not be hit easily in the body. Connolly was still flailing with his telegraphed lefts and rights but he was missing much more often than he landed. Sweat was coursing down his blood-soaked face and guttural noises were coming from between his shattered front teeth.

Connolly missed with another flailing hook and pulled up in his following run to launch a ferocious kick at McLure's groin. McLure grabbed at the big man's foot and twisted it with both hands, sending Connolly tumbling to the sawdust-strewn floor. The giant struggled back slowly to his feet, shaking his head, the resolution starting to flow out of him.

McLure went straight at him for the kill. He threw a left hook, deliberately missed and then brought his elbow back smashing against Connolly's jaw. Connolly went down like a puppet whose strings had been released. He still managed to crawl back on to his hands and knees and glared im-potently up at McLure. Then his head jerked back despairingly as McLure brought his foot smashing against his chin. Connolly rolled over on to his side and lay still.

McLure staggered back, just as four of the uniformed Confederate soldiers cut out a wedge across the saloon floor towards him, hickory sticks clutched in their hands. Efficiently they closed in on McLure from different sides. He managed to drop one with a short hook to the jaw but then had to throw up his hands to protect his head and shoulders against the rain of blows descending upon him. There was a sudden explosion in his skull and then he was falling swiftly into a dark and bottomless hole.

FOUR

When McLure came round he was lying on an iron bunk chained to the wall in one of the cells of the sheriff's office. He staggered off a filthy, straw padded mattress and made his way unsteadily towards the bars of the heavy, iron-barred door. His head was whirling and his legs were finding difficulty in supporting his weight.

Duvall, the Confederate captain who seemed to fill the post of town marshal, looked up from some paperwork on his desk.

'Didn't take you long to land here,' he said curtly. 'You've been fined a hundred dollars for breaching the peace. The money's been took from your pocket. You're going to have to sweat it out here until tomorrow morning. If you want breakfast then it'll be another ten dollars.'

McLure's hand flew to the breast pocket of his shirt. The remains of his depleted bankroll felt even slimmer. At this rate he would only be able to afford another couple of days in the town. He would have to expedite matters.

'Hell, it was just a fight,' he grumbled morosely.

'You took on the orniest *hombre* in the town,' commented Duvall, a trace of reluctant respect shading his tone. 'We've done you a favour bringing you in, before you decided to go up into the hills looking for a couple of grizzlies to annoy.'

'He wasn't so tough,' lied McLure, ignoring the screaming evidence of his aching limbs and throbbing head.

Duvall stood up and walked over to the cell. 'What is it with you?' he demanded with genuine curiosity. 'Most bindle-stiffs who end up here are only too willing to keep out of trouble. You seem to go looking for it.'

'I don't back away from nothing,' said McLure bellicosely, choosing his words with care. He wanted to give the impression of a man of courage and resource but he had to be careful not to overdo it, in case the others became suspicious.

'Then you're crazy,' said Duvall dismissively. 'You cause any more trouble in this town and Major Glanville's going to have to deal with you personally.'

It was the first time that Duvall had heard Glanville's name mentioned since he had ridden into the town. He felt a tingling at the back of his neck. Involuntarily he clenched his fists. He forced himself to look casual.

'Who's this Glanville?' he asked.

'Major Glanville runs Slaughter City,' said Duvall. 'That's all you need to know. Better pray you never run across him.'

The two sergeants who appeared to act as Duvall's deputies swaggered in noisily from the street. Duvall walked away from the cell door and exchanged a few terse words in an undertone with them. He picked up a shotgun from a rack on the wall. Without looking back at McLure he went out into the street and walked briskly away. One of the sergeants slumped into the chair behind the desk, while the other stood staring idly out of the window. Neither man paid any attention to the prisoner.

They had had it too easy, thought McLure. They were so sure of their supremity in the town they no longer even expected anything to go belly-up. Well, it was up to him to prove them wrong. At least the sergeants should be easier to outwit than the wily Duvall. On the other hand there were two of the NCOs, so he would have to be careful.

He surveyed the tiny cell. Apart from the barred door the only other way out was through a small window set high in the wall. In his days as a marshal he had deposited hundreds of prisoners in similar surroundings. He had also witnessed their occasional methods of trying to escape. There had been one particularly successful attempt on the part of a resourceful bank robber in Arkansas just before the war. McLure had admired the man's gall even as he had brought him down with a snap shot to the leg when the bank robber had fled up the street. Now he was going to try the same idea.

Keeping a wary eye on his gaolers, he sat on the straw mattress on his bunk and took off one boot. He transferred the three white-headed phosphorous matches he had secreted there earlier in the day to his pants pocket. Still watching the two sergeants, he reached up inside his shirt and took out the small muslin packet from the strapping. If the non-coms had instituted a proper search of his person when he had been brought in they would have found the contraband. He had based his plan on the fact that he would almost certainly have been unconscious when he had been carried to the gaol, patently presenting a threat to no one.

He struck one of the matches against the wall and tossed it on to the straw protruding from the holes in the mattress. There was a brief crackle and the fire took hold. Almost at once the mattress was ablaze, sending out clouds of black smoke which filled the cell.

McLure hesitated and then threw the packet on to the flames. In the same moment he hurled himself on to the floor against the far wall, covering his head with his hands.

He had instructed Pinkerton to add a little extra saltpetre to the black powder compressed in the packet, in order to increase the noise of the explosion caused by the celebrated bang-juice used in mining operations. For a moment he thought that the Scot had overdone it. The blast from the reaction of the powder to the flames rocked the cell, almost deafening him. The acrid smoke continued to billow from the mattress, obscuring the view of the guards.

'Help!' bellowed McLure, trying to endow his voice with the necessary element of panic. 'I'm on fire! Someone's trying to blow the place up!'

Through the smoke he could just about make out the blundering forms of the panic-stricken non-coms. McLure screamed again.

'I'm on fire!' he yelled. 'Do something about it! Let me out!'

'Go round the back!' one of the guards shouted to the other, belatedly taking charge. 'See who threw that explosive through the cell window.'

McLure watched one of the sergeants lumbering out of the front door. The second man felt his way cautiously through the smoke to the cell and peered indecisively through the bars. McLure writhed in simulated agony on the floor.

'Get me to a doctor,' he begged.

'Hold on,' grunted the other man, struggling with a bunch of keys. 'I'll soon have you out.'

He hesitated and then seemed to have second thoughts. He lumbered away and took a metal cash-box from a drawer in the desk. Carefully he placed it high on a shelf well away from the billowing flames.

'Get a move on!' shouted McLure.

'Hold your horses,' spat the non-com, returning to the cell. He turned a key in the lock and swung the door open. The smoke was so thick that he could hardly make out the form of the groaning prisoner. He reached McLure and bent over him. It was what McLure had been waiting for. He swung a desperate roundhouse right up at his gaoler. It connected on the sergeant's stubbly chin. The non-com grunted and staggered back dazedly. McLure propelled himself to his feet and hit the staggering sergeant twice more to the head with swinging lefts and rights. The non-com went down like a sack of grain falling from a wagon.

Pausing only to take the unconscious man's Colt from his holster, McLure headed for the door. He could hear confused shouts coming from the street but night had fallen and he should have a chance of getting to the end of the street and the livery stable in the confusion. He hurried out of the door into the cool night air and sprinted towards the stable.

'Hold it!'

McLure stopped. Duvall was standing in front of him, the barrel of a shotgun pointed towards McLure's stomach.

FIVE

Duvall escorted McLure back into the marshal's office, prodding him forward with his shotgun. The fire in the cell had been doused with water by the first non-com and was smouldering sullenly. The non-com knocked out by McLure during his escape bid had staggered back to his feet. He was replacing the cash-box in the desk drawer. When he saw the big man he swore violently and bulled his way across the room to drive his fist viciously into McLure's face. McLure's head jolted back and he could taste the salt blood trickling from his lips. The sergeant balled his fist again and drew it back.

'That's enough!' The order cracked like a whip across the room.

McLure and the non-com turned. Another man was standing in the doorway. He was tall and broad-shouldered, in a black swallow-tail coat, frilled shirt and fancy tie. The man had a wide, pleasant face surmounted by a head of tight black curls. There was a sheen of good living on him; this was a man who seldom missed meals and usually slept in a soft bed. He possessed an air of easy authority. He would be the best of bar-room company, full of Irish affability, judged McLure, and equally one who could also turn on you as quickly and as viciously as a rattlesnake. The newcomer was surveying him with frank curiosity.

'This the guy who whipped Connolly last night?' he asked amiably.

'He just made a break for it,' whined the non-com, feeling his bruised jaw ruefully. 'Got out of his cell and high-tailed it away. If Duvall hadn't been coming along he might have made it.'

'He wouldn't have made it,' said the newcomer, advancing into the office with assurance. 'He never meant to. He just wanted to make you guys look what you are

– a bunch of brainless saddle-tramps.'

'What are you saying, Glanville?' asked Duvall, flushing.

McLure stiffened. He tried to school his face to remain expressionless. So this was the man who had led his company out of the line to safety at Shiloh and allowed the Yankees to outflank the Confederate forces and decimate his regiment. And this was the man he had sworn to kill. If he had had a weapon he would have used it here and now and taken the consequences. With an effort McLure fought down his rage.

'I'm saying that only a fool would pick a fight with Connolly and then try to bust out of gaol,' said Glanville patiently, as if talking to a child. 'And whatever else he might be this guy's no fool. Soon as I heard about the fight and the gaol-break I thought I'd better come along and give him the once-over.' He drew closer to McLure, his shrewd brown eyes raking the other man's face.

'What's the idea, big fella? You deliberately trying to make my guys look bad?'

'Wasn't difficult,' said McLure tersely.

'Ain't that the truth,' sighed Glanville. 'You just can't get the hired help these days.'

'What's going on here?' blustered Duvall uncomfortably. 'McLure's just another bum drifting through Slautara.'

'He's a hell of a sight more than that,' murmured Glanville, his soft brown eyes still summing McLure up. 'Whether that's good or bad for us remains to be seen.'

McLure felt an ominous tightening at the back of his throat. Surely Glanville could not suspect his true mission in the town already? There was only one way to find out.

'That's right,' he said, with a confidence that he was far from feeling. 'I heard you had a sweet deal here in Slaughter City. Figured you might need a good man.'

'Nobody needs you,' snarled Duvall. 'Mister, all you're buying is a one-way ticket to Boot Hill.'

'You reckon you could make it here, do you?' asked Glanville, a smile playing about the corner of his lips. 'You've got gall, I'll grant you that.'

'Try me,' suggested McLure.

'Don't listen to him Glanville!' burst out an incensed Duvall. 'He wants my job!'

'Is that all?' drawled Glanville, appearing to be amused by the situation. 'That's all right then. For a minute I thought he wanted mine.'

'You going to let him get away with this?' demanded Duvall wildly.

Glanville shrugged. 'The way I see it, you're the one in trouble, Pete,' he chuckled. 'It's your fight, you deal with it.'

'It's your fight too,' said McLure.

'Well now, how do you make that out?' asked Glanville lightly.

'Duvall and his two side-kicks are dealing to you from the bottom of the pack,' McLure told him. 'Every time a drifter pays the town tax, they take a cut for themselves.'

'Don't pay no never-mind to him!' shouted Duvall furiously. 'He's just rousting you, Glanville.'

'Hush now, Pete,' said Glanville lightly,

but his gaze was suddenly serious. He turned to McLure. 'How do you make that out, stranger?'

'Saw it with my own eyes,' said McLure evenly. 'When they took my wad after I first came here, they divided it into two piles, not one. That first gave me the idea. Then when I set my cell on fire this morning the first thing one of the deputies did was to rescue a cash-box from the desk drawer. That made me think that they were probably running their own deal without you knowing.'

'Are you going to listen to this?' demanded Duvall hoarsely, but there was fear in his tone.

'Take a look,' suggested McLure. 'They've put the box back in the drawer.'

'Well now, that would seem to be a fair solution,' nodded Glanville. His eyes were hooded, like a snake's before it struck. He nodded to the first non-com. 'Joe, you slide that drawer out nice and easy, and take out whatever you find inside.'

The non-com looked confusedly at Duvall.

70

The marshal ignored him, glaring male-volently at McLure. The non-com shrugged and slid open the desk drawer. He took out the cashbox to reveal a mass of banknotes and a number of pieces of jewellery.

'That ring on top was took from me when I came into Slautara yesterday,' said McLure.

'Is that a fact?' asked Glanville coolly. 'And there was you, Pete, assuring me only last night that you had turned over the day's takings to me. Looks like you've been holding out on me. What I'm wondering is, how long has this been going on?'

Duvall snarled at McLure. His arm snaked for the Colt in his holster. In the same movement, Glanville flipped a Smith & Wesson belly pistol from his waistband over to McLure. The Colt roared. McLure felt the slug tear into his upper arm. He controlled the belly pistol and snapped off one shot. It caught Duvall in the throat. The marshal staggered back, blood gushing out. He fell to the floor in a flurry of arms and legs and then lay still, blood pumping furiously from his neck.

Glanville had stooped and drawn a derringer from his sock and was facing down the two startled non-coms.

'True, it's only got one shot,' he informed them softly. 'Do you want to take your chances on which one of you I kill with it?'

The two deputies hesitated and then shook their heads sullenly. Glanville gestured to the still smoking cell.

'I think I'll have you both in there until I decide what to do with you,' he said. 'In you get, boys.'

The two hang-dog non-coms shuffled into the cell. Glanville took a key from a hook on the wall and turned it in the lock. Then he looked at McLure, caressing his chin thoughtfully with one hand.

'Well now,' he mused aloud. 'I didn't order this from no menu, that's for sure. We'd better get you to the doc, so that he can take a look at that wound. And as it might be said that I owe you one, I'll even pay the bill myself.'

SIX

A gawping, shuffling crowd had gathered outside the marshal's office hoping for more action by the time Glanville led McLure out into the street. Half-a-dozen armed and worried-looking deputies in Confederate uniforms were converging at the run on the building from different directions. Glanville paused briefly to give them instructions about dispersing the mob and calling the coldmeat wagon to dispose of Duvall's corpse. He ordered that the possessions of the two imprisoned deputies should be impounded before they were run out of town. Then he took McLure briskly along the main street.

'We'll get you fixed up in no time,' he promised confidently.

'Ain't nothing but a flesh wound,'

protested McLure, following the other man.

'I know it. All the same, I want you healed fast. I've got work for you to do.'

'What sort of work?' asked McLure.

'You'll find out,' came the reply.

McLure hurried to keep up. 'Why did you throw me the belly gun in there?' he asked.

'I wanted to see if you had the salt to kill a man,' replied Glanville briefly. 'Well, you sure did.'

He stopped outside a small, neat clapboard house at the end of the street and rapped on the door. After a few moments it was opened by a young woman in a calico dress and spotless white apron. She was in her late twenties with dark eyes that were reserved and watchful. He face was oval in shape and delicate.

''Morning, Nora,' Glanville greeted her cheerfully. 'Doc Bernes in?'

'He's busy, Mr Glanville,' said the woman quietly.

'Still drunk, you mean,' said Glanville. 'That's all right; you do most of his work for him anyway. I want you to fix up a friend of mine. This is McLure. Don't know his first name. McLure, this is Mrs Nora Wright, the town nurse and regular stand-in doctor.'

For the first time the girl's eyes travelled beyond Glanville to take in his companion. McLure touched his hat.

'Greg McLure,' he said. 'Pleased to meet you, ma'am.'

'You're hurt, Mr McLure,' said the girl, flushing a little under his steady scrutiny. She opened the door wider. 'Come through to the office.'

She led them into the doctor's office. It was sparsely furnished, with a camp bed in one corner. On a shelf were bottles and jars of opium pills, calomel and quinine. McLure knew that somewhere out of sight would be stored the meat saws and hot irons ready to be adapted by the doctor for his work.

'Take off your shirt, please Mr McLure,' said Nora.

Glanville helped McLure off with his shirt. Nora looked closely at the wound, her delicate fingers working lightly on his arm.

'The bullet went right through the fleshy part,' she said after a moment's investigation. 'No great harm done. Do you want me to deal with it, or would you rather wait until Doc Bernes gets up?'

There was an air of understated cool confidence about the young woman which impelled trust in others. McLure nodded.

'You go ahead, Mrs Wright,' he said.

'Good choice,' said Glanville, chuckling throatily.

With deft fingers the woman cleaned out the wound before taking a needle and thread from a drawer and proceeding to stitch up the arm. Her movements were economical and efficient.

'Where's the man who shot you?' she asked expressionlessly, her fingers working busily. 'Will I have another patient soon?'

'Not this time,' said Granville. 'He was last seen headed feet-first for Boot Hill.'

Nora's lips compressed at the levity in the other man's tone, but she kept her head bowed as she continued with her suturing. 'Are you a gunman, Mr McLure?' she asked with evident distaste as she worked.

'No,' said McLure tersely.

'Then where did you learn to shoot like that?' asked Glanville. 'I've been wondering that myself.'

'I was a lawman before the war,' said McLure. He tried not to put too much emphasis on the information. He wanted to start Glanville's thoughts moving in a certain direction, but he did not want to be too direct about it. To his relief the other man seemed to rise to the bait.

'Where?' asked Glanville, looking interested.

'Bodine,' said McLure.

Glanville whistled. 'Tough town,' he commented. 'You were lucky to survive.'

'Luck had nothing to do with it,' said McLure.

'No, maybe not,' conceded Glanville. 'You'd need a brain or two as well.'

'Is that how you've survived the war, Mr

McLure?' asked Nora contemptuously, concentrating on closing up the wound in her patient's upper arm. 'Did you have the brains to ride away from it, like so many others around here?'

McLure was startled by the sudden vehemence of the woman's attack. Before he could answer, Glanville spoke.

'Now then, Nora,' he said hastily. 'You know none of us in Slaughter City discuss the war. It's none of our concern. You'll have to excuse Mrs Wright, Greg. She lost her husband at Gettysburg.'

'I'm sorry to hear that, ma'am,' said McLure sincerely.

'He didn't have enough brains, you see, Mr McLure,' said Nora, stepping back and surveying her handiwork dispassionately. 'He stayed on and fought to the death.'

There was an awkward pause in the small room. Then Nora threw McLure's blood-stained shirt back at him.

'I'm done,' she said.

'Thank you, Nora,' said Glanville

smoothly, as if there had never been any unpleasantness. 'I'll settle up with Doc Bernes the next time I see him.'

The young woman nodded without speaking. McLure muttered his thanks. 'Don't suppose I'll be seeing you again,' he added awkwardly. 'My rent money's nearly run out. I'll be leaving Slautara tomorrow or the next day.'

'Forget that,' said Glanville expansively, clapping McLure on the back. 'I ain't going to let a potent handful like you ride away. Men with guts and brains are in short supply in these parts. How would you like Pete Duvall's job?'

'What, town marshal?' asked McLure, genuine surprise in his tone. At most he had been hoping to work himself forward to be offered a deputy's job.

'Why not?' shrugged Glanville. 'Like you said, you've been a lawman before. The only difference is that this time you'll answer to me, not a town committee. And the pay's better. I'll run to fifty bucks a week and your keep. All you've got to do is ride shotgun on the town for me, while I concentrate on more important matters. Won't be easy, mind. What do you say?'

'All right,' said McLure, attempting to seem dubious. 'I'll give it a shot.'

'Just one thing,' warned Glanville. 'When you put in with me, you come along for the whole ride. I'll pay you well and look after you, but I don't allow any of my deputies to leave Slaughter City – not for any reason. That all right with you?'

'Suits me just fine,' nodded McLure.

'Good man,' enthused Glanville. 'Come on, I'll introduce you to your deputies.'

'You bastards!' spat Nora Wright.

McLure turned in surprise. The nurse was standing pale and shaken by the table. She was glaring vindictively at both men. Glanville looked sheepish.

'It had to happen one day,' he said, spreading his hands wide. 'Duvall was a mite slow on the draw for a man with his ambitions. Sooner or later he was bound to come up against a faster man.'

'And you bring that killer to me to be patched up,' said Nora, still trembling. 'Glanville, you're an evil man.'

'What's going on here?' asked McLure. He looked from Glanville to Nora. The man was grinning slightly, while the woman was still white and rigid.

'I thought it best not to tell you while you were still in need of attention,' said Glanville, not taking his speculative eyes from Nora.

'Tell me what?' asked McLure.

'Well, you see,' said Glanville, unmoved, easing McLure out of the house into the street. 'Nora was Pete Duvall's woman.'

'The hell she was,' said McLure, stopping, aghast at the news. 'Then why did you take me to her to get patched up?'

'You'd have to have met her sooner or later,' shrugged Glanville. 'You're my new marshal and Nora's important to me, not just because she's one prime woman, but also because she keeps the town healthy.

Come on, I'm going to put you to work.'

McLure followed Glanville down the street. He was still trying to work out why the town boss had insisted on the unnecessary and hurtful encounter with the young woman. He could only put it down to Glanville's nature. Plainly he was the sort of man who liked stirring the stew pot just to see what floated to the top. There was no doubt about it: Glanville was an unpredictable and unscrupulous man.

And dangerous with it.

SEVEN

The next two weeks of Greg McLure's life were among the busiest he had ever spent. Glanville had been right; the job was not easy. In addition to controlling the outlaws and renegades buying sanctuary in the town, McLure had to exact the town tax from newcomers and take it over to Glanville at the end of each day. He also had to assert control over the twenty or so Confederate non-coms who served as deputies, working shifts round the clock in the streets, working as outriders around the town and searching and taxing any new arrivals.

Not all of the marshal's assistants had taken easily to McLure's promotion over their heads, despite Glanville's solid endorsement. There were those among them who resented his easy rise to his new position and gave it as their considered opinion that the new marshal could fall into a pile of buffalo chips and still come up smelling like a rambler rose. However, after McLure had thrashed two of them in fist-fights and pistol-whipped a third for being found asleep on duty he had secured their grudging respect, if not their liking.

There was only one bright spot on the horizon as far as McLure was concerned: this was Seb Wiley, the chief deputy, a thickset, undemonstrative character, poker-faced, slow to speak but even slower to back off from trouble. McLure knew nothing of the man's background but his value had soon become apparent. Unlike most of the deputies Wiley could think for himself and could be relied upon to finish off any task given to him without fuss. He was also one of the best shots with revolver and rifle that McLure had ever seen. Within a short time McLure had grown to depend upon his taciturn chief assistant.

He needed all the help he could get. It was

the outlaw element of Slaughter City which occupied most of McLure's time and attention during those early days. So many newcomers were drifting into the town that it seemed as if Pinkerton had been correct in his forecast that the war was edging to its exhausted close.

The news brought with the latest arrivals confirmed this. Sherman's army had cut a swathe sixty miles wide to the sea, fulfilling his threat to make Georgia howl. Grant was making a final assault on Lee's force guarding Richmond. The South was awash with deserters, outlaws and freed slaves. There was no law left anywhere in the Southern states.

Except in Slaughter City. With the dogged assistance of Wiley, McLure saw to that. In a two-week period they disarmed, faced down and controlled the rabble of road-agents, rustlers, looters and gamblers taking up temporary abode in Slautara. Among the latest arrivals were desperate guerrillas who had ridden with Quantrill and Bloody Bill

Anderson. General Grant himself had already announced that there would be no pardon for the men who had massacred the inhabitants of Lawrence and other Kansas border towns.

McLure admitted them to Slautara – as long as they could pay. He spent most of his waking hours patrolling the streets, making sure that the scum within the city limits walked quietly. They were encouraged to reprovision at exorbitant rates in the local stores, buy their pleasure in the bawdy houses and to gamble away what was left at the faro tables. Then, when the period of sanctuary purchased by each man had elapsed, McLure and Wiley and the other deputies escorted the outlaws and their hangers-on out of town.

Most of them grumbled, a few tried to make a play with their newly returned guns, until they discovered that the chambers were empty. These men were dragged from their mounts and thrashed, as a sign that in Slaughter City, Greg McLure's word was, in every sense, now the law.

One or two of the beaten men threatened to return, but the knowledge that Slautara had once repelled a whole Union Army company was enough to contain their threats to a few muttered and impotent growls as they spurred their mounts savagely away.

Another of McLure's duties was to carry the day's income to Glanville in his hotel room. The money consisted of the tax levied on that day's arrivals, together with a percentage of the takings of the brothels, saloons, stores and gambling halls. Under McLure's protection these establishments were making so much profit with so little effort that there were only a few token protests at the nightly twenty per cent extracted by the brusque, lean-faced new marshal with the wide shoulders and the big reputation.

'Greg, my man, this is Christmas in March,' chuckled Glanville contentedly one night after he had finished counting the contents of the bulging saddle-bags carried over by McLure. He entered the total with a turkey quill on a rough sheet of paper and then poured the other man a shot of rye. 'I knew Duvall was dealing himself a few cards off the bottom, but I didn't know the scale of it, until I got myself an honest marshal.'

'It won't last for ever,' McLure warned him. 'War'll be over in a few weeks. Then President Lincoln will have time to think about places like Slautara.'

'I know it,' said Glanville calmly. 'He's sent in his agents to close the place down before now. Doesn't bother me none. Slaughter City is just a side-show as far as I'm concerned. Set up to earn me a little seed-corn money I've got something bigger planned. Much bigger.'

'What's that?' asked McLure, trying not to sound too eager but wondering if at last he would learn something.

Glanville winked and refilled his glass. 'I want you to report here again at sun-up tomorrow morning,' he said evasively. 'We're going for a ride.'

'Too much to expect you to tell me where, I suppose,' said McLure, taking the hint and rising to go.

Glanville winked and refilled his glass. 'I like you fine, Greg,' he said expansively. 'But I still don't tell you everything.'

You don't tell me hardly anything, thought McLure bitterly as he left the hotel and stepped out into the gloom. For all his gregarious temperament Glanville played his cards very close to his vest.

His path back to his hotel room took him past the doctor's house. The curved white quarter moon had disappeared behind a cloud and it was hard to see anything, even though lamps were burning in a few small windows. The few men and women who passed him were little more than shadows scudding across the ground.

There was a sharp crack and something seemed to tug fiercely at the sleeve of his shirt. McLure hurled himself to the ground, squirming round on to his stomach and at the same time drawing his Colt. Everything was silent again. The shadows in the street had disappeared, gone to ground or scattering for the safety of the shadows of the buildings. For a moment McLure wondered if he could have been mistaken. With his free hand he groped for his sleeve. The cloth was tattered and torn and was smoking slightly. He had not been wrong. Someone had taken a shot at him and missed by less than an inch. Cautiously McLure climbed to his feet. Two more shots rang out. McLure could hear their impact in the dust close to his feet. He fired back automatically in the direction of the flashes coming from his assailant's pistol. There was a pause and then he heard the sound of feet running away through the night. McLure raced in their direction.

The man seemed to be heading for the livery stables in a side alley off the main street. McLure abandoned caution and increased his pace before the man was lost amid the side streets. For a moment he wondered if he had lost his man but then he saw a dim outline of a form backing into the stables.

'What's going on?' demanded Glanville's voice. The town boss appeared at McLure's elbow. He was holding a carbine in his arms.

'Somebody bushwhacked me,' McLure informed him. 'He's just gone into the stables. I'm going after him.'

'Wait!' ordered Glanville. He jerked his head at the empty street behind him. 'The deputies should be here any minute. Wait until they arrive.'

McLure hesitated but saw the point in the other man's suggestion. Inside a couple of minutes half-a-dozen armed deputies came running up the street, alerted by the sudden burst of gunfire. In a few words the marshal told them what had happened.

'Three of you go round in back of the stables,' he ordered. 'Scott, Banner, you come in after me through the front.' He looked round. 'Where's Wiley?'

'He's already gone round the back,' one of the deputies informed him.

McLure nodded. Wiley was experienced enough not to need any instructions. He only hoped the younger deputies would be as dependable. Taking a deep breath he broke into a trot and shouldered his way into the livery stables. Two shots rang out from the far side. McLure dived to the straw-covered ground, at the same time loosing off three shots of his own. There was a sharp cry from the gloom, followed by the dull thud of a body falling.

'Fan out!' ordered McLure sharply, easing himself to his feet as the deputies spread into a line on either side of him. Cautiously he advanced into the stables. There were horse-boxes on either side. Frightened by the noise of the firing, their occupants were rearing and whinnying. McLure screwed up his eyes in an effort to make some sense out of the shadows before him. It sounded as if he had shot his assailant, but the man might still be alive and waiting to reply in a deadly kind.

'Good shooting in the dark,' commented

Glanville, moving carefully up on to McLure's shoulder. 'You couldn't have seen anything.'

'I fired at the flashes,' said McLure, not relaxing. 'He should be ahead of us somewhere.'

An excited shout from one of the deputies alerted them to the presence of the body. McLure surged forward with the others. Discarding caution Glanville took the lead. There was the form of a man slumped against the far wall of the stable. It was too dark for McLure to make out who it was. Glanville knelt at the man's side. When he looked up there was alarm and concern in the town boss's voice.

'For God's sake, McLure!' he snarled accusingly. 'You've shot Seb Wiley!'

EIGHT

'The streets are clear,' said McLure coming back into the livery stables with half-a-dozen deputies. 'There's no sign of any gunman. A few rubberneckers from the saloons are beginning to gather. I've got Scott and Banner keeping 'em back.' He looked at the figure slumped against the wall. A dark wet patch stained the front of the man's shirt. 'How's Wiley?'

'Not good,' said Glanville glancing up. Someone had brought a lantern and placed it on the straw. It was still difficult to see by its fitful light. 'I've sent for Doc Bernes.' He waved the advancing McLure back. 'Keep away and give him room, all of you.'

The deputies edged back. McLure was aware that none of them would meet his gaze. It did not do much for their confidence when the marshal gunned down his own chief assistant. McLure could not imagine how he had come to make such a mistake. He had fired through the gloom at the flashes coming from the pistol of the man who had been trying to kill him. Somehow the senior deputy had got in the way. McLure felt sick.

The batwing doors of the stables clattered open again and Nora Wright swept in, clutching the battered carpet bag in which she kept her nursing accoutrements. She looked briefly at McLure but did not acknowledge his existence.

'I wanted the doc,' growled Glanville.

'Then you'll have to make do with me,' said Nora briefly, kneeling next to Glanville at the wounded man's side. 'Doc's gone to bed with a bottle or three. Believe me, you don't want him tending anyone tonight. What happened to Seb?'

'The marshal shot him by mistake,' said one of the younger deputies before Glanville could glare him into resentful silence.

'Is that so?' asked Nora drily, pausing in her ministrations to glance up at the silent McLure. 'I sure don't need fire, flood nor pestilence to bring me my patients,' she went on, turning back to the bloodstained man. 'I could hire you full-time to provide them, Marshal McLure.'

'Never mind the jokes. How is he?' asked Glanville impatiently.

Nora shook her head. 'Bad,' she said tersely. 'As far as I can tell he's taken two shots to the chest. He's lost a lot of blood and his lungs may be punctured. I'm doing my best to stop the bleeding, but in the long term he'll need better help than Doc Bernes and I can provide here. We've got to get him to a properly-equipped hospital with qualified surgeons, and we've got to do it fast.'

'Maddox City,' said Glanville without hesitation. 'It's forty miles away, but they've got everything Wiley will need there. They won't ask any questions either, as long as he's got enough money with him.' He turned to one of the younger deputies. 'Kearns, there's a covered wagon over there. Hitch a team of mules to it and take two horses on lead-ropes with you, and take Wiley to Maddox. Make sure the wagon's well provisioned before you leave.' The deputy hesitated. Impatiently Glanville took a handful of gold pieces from his coat pocket and handed them to the young man. 'Pay the doctors what it takes and keep the rest for yourself. Then get back here as fast as you can. As soon as you reach Maddox, pay a messenger to ride over and tell me so.'

'Yes, sir,' said Kearns with alacrity, thrusting the heavy coins into his pocket, and running to the stalls.

'It's a rough journey to Maddox,' said Nora, standing. 'He'll need someone to look after him on the way.'

'You go with him then,' said Glanville absently. 'Come back with Kearns after.'

'I've got work to do in Slautara,' protested Nora.

'You're only in Slaughter City on my say-so,' replied Glanville sharply. 'If you want to stay, ma'am, you'd better do as I say. Go and pack a bag and be ready to leave with Kearns and Wiley in half an hour.'

Nora bit her lip to keep back her objections. She turned and started ministering to the wounded man. Glanville gestured to the deputies.

'Give Kearns a hand to hitch the wagon,' he ordered. 'Then put some straw on the floor for Wiley.'

The others turned away at once to do his bidding. McLure made as if to approach Wiley again. Once more Glanville restrained him. 'Get out of here now,' he said urgently in a low voice. 'You ain't none too popular with the deputies. As long as they see you standing around they'll be reminded of what you did to Wiley. Let everyone sleep on it.'

McLure nodded reluctantly. 'I still can't figure out how I shot him,' he said. 'I fired at the one who was shooting at me, I swear it.'

'We'll talk about it tomorrow,' said Glanville abstractedly, watching the deputies pulling the covered wagon and the horses into place. 'Meet me outside the hotel at sun-up. We'll get out of town for a couple of hours and talk it over.'

'I sure hope Wiley's going to be all right,' said McLure anxiously, heading for the door.

'So do they,' said Glanville callously, indicating the struggling deputies as they manipulated the cumbersome wagon into position. 'That's two of their kind you've shot already since you've been in Slaughter City. They wouldn't want it to get to be a habit!'

He walked ahead out of the livery stable with McLure. The other deputies had made a good job of clearing away the crowd because, apart from a few of the tethered horses belonging to the deputies, the streets were empty again. McLure felt sick and weary. He had had no intention of killing Wiley or any of the other deputies. Glanville had always been his prey, and here he was alone with the town boss. McLure knew that this would be as good a time as any to gun Glanville down. He could do it, take one of the horses from the hitching rail and be out of Slautara before anyone could do anything about it.

The town boss was still talking as they walked down the street, lit only by pale stars. McLure knew that he could not shoot Glanville in the back. He had to call him and give the man a fair chance. He stopped walking and set himself, his hand hovering over his holster. Glanville walked on, oblivious to what was happening. McLure made his decision. He crouched and opened his mouth to call upon the man he hated to turn and draw.

The door of the livery stable opened and Nora stepped out into the street. Her eyes took in the scene. McLure relaxed, dropping his hand to his side. The time for killing had passed as quickly and silently as the flight of a small bird. Glanville heard the sound of the door and turned.

'Have I been talking to myself?' he demanded in surprise.

'Just catching up with you,' McLure told him.

'I'm going to pack a bag,' said Nora, passing without looking at either man.

McLure looked after the young woman. He wondered just how much she had seen and what she had made of that silent tableau in the night street.

NINE

McLure saddled up and rode to Glanville's hotel soon after sun-up the following morning. To his surprise the other man was already waiting for him by the hitching rail outside the front entrance. For once the big man had discarded his city suit. He was wearing Levis and a thick coarse shirt. A heavy Smith & Wesson .44 was strapped to his leg, while a Remington rifle jutted from a saddle holster on his pinto.

The big man was not displaying his usual spurious affability either. He greeted McLure with a brief nod, untethered his mount from the hitching rail and at once swung into his saddle, heading out of town, past the respectful guards at the entrance and posted on the mesa above the town.

'We'll go south later,' Glanville told his

companion. 'I don't want anyone in the town seeing which way we're heading.' McLure rode in silence at Glanville's side as they trotted their mounts across the plain, skirting a gaping, jagged hole some forty feet across. Glanville followed the direction of his companion's gaze.

'We blew a few of Abe's boys to glory here once,' he grunted with satisfaction.

And before that you deserted your own kind when you saved your neck at Shiloh, thought McLure, a surge of pure hatred coursing through his veins.

'How far do you think Wiley will have got by now?' he asked, bringing up the subject which had hardly left his mind for the past ten hours.

Glanville shrugged callously. 'A third of the way to Maddox, or all the way to Hell, I'd say,' he replied.

They rode for three hours, at first following an abandoned wagon-route and gradually leaving the flat plain behind them and guiding their mounts through the buffalo grass and the rising scrub-dotted foothills. Glanville led the way upwards with the easy confidence of a man who had covered the ground many times before. By mid-morning they were gentling their horses at a comfortable single-foot pace along a wooded plateau overlooking the flat-lands below. A hawk circled and dropped and a wolf howled once far away. At a sign from Glanville they dismounted and tied their reins to the branches of a stunted tree. They watered their horses out of their hats and drank from their remaining canteen. Then they loosed the cinches on their mounts to let them blow.

'Best to keep as quiet as a new fall of snow,' whispered the big man. 'We'll just take a look over the edge.'

He led the way to the lip of the plateau and stared down intently. McLure stood at his shoulder. Far below on the plain, ant-like in their size and industry, a mixture of Union soldiers and shirt-sleeved civilian contractors were working with pick-axes, crow-bars and hand-drills on a shattered wrought-iron railroad line, hammering in fresh spikes and trying to straighten out and reinforce the twisted metal. Behind them, as far as the eye could see, lay miles of repaired track, but there was just as much deformed metal ahead of them still awaiting repair. New spikes and rails were being brought up in trucks pulled by a team of horses along the repaired sections of the track, before the horses were re-tethered to the far end of the now empty trucks and taken back until they disappeared into the distance. A dozen men were lifting each new rail into position on to the tops of the sleepers. Other workers drove in the spikes, flattened the earth with spades and bolted the lines together.

'A year ago, the Union boys blew up the track to stop Robert E. Lee from using it,' said Glanville softly, his eyes intent on the frenzied activity below. 'Which is something of a shame when you consider that there ain't above a dozen railroad tracks in the whole of Texas yet, most of 'em going from nowhere to noplace. Now they're busy mending this line again.'

'What for?' asked McLure.

'Why, for us, Greg,' murmured Glanville, expansive again, as if his spirits had been lifted by what he had seen. 'For us, of course. Ain't that nice of them?'

He clapped the other man on the shoulder with a guffaw and turned and returned to their mounts.

As they cantered back towards the town McLure wondered what Glanville was up to and why he had insisted on bringing company to the site. He dropped back slightly until he had a view of the big man's broad back. It would be only too easy to draw his Colt and shoot the renegade here and now, he thought. That would solve all his problems and allow him to ride away in safety. True Pinkerton would be annoyed, because he wanted Slaughter City destroyed as well as having its boss killed. But what did he care about Pinkerton? Slowly McLure's hand began to drop on to the handle of his Colt.

'What did you think when you saw them Yankee uniforms down on the plain?' asked Glanville suddenly.

He glanced back casually over his shoulder and eased his speed until they were riding side by side again. Unobtrusively, McLure returned his grip from his Colt to the reins.

'I fought 'em for two years,' he said shortly. 'How do you expect me to feel?'

'That's the big difference between us, Greg,' said Glanville, as if talking to an obtuse child. 'I fought 'em too – for a while. But they were never the enemy to me, just a nuisance. That's why I rode away from the fighting sooner than you probably did. I don't mind fighting, as long as I get paid well enough. So now I'm coming back to it because it's likely to show a profit.'

'What profit?' asked McLure. 'And where do I come in?'

'What I had in mind,' said Glanville carefully, 'was going to involve Pete Duvall and maybe half a dozen of his deputies. Only you killed Duvall and showed me that the others weren't worth a pitcher of warm spit. Now I reckon the pair of us and maybe two of the deputies can do it together.'

'Do what?' asked McLure, interested in spite of himself. Glanville was a clever man, there was no doubt about that. Any scheme that he had worked out would probably be ingenious enough to be worth listening to.

'What's the plan?' he asked.

'I'll come to that,' Glanville assured him. 'First, you tell me: are you ready to come in with me? It'll be hard and dangerous, but if we pull it off we'll both be rich.'

'Always had a hankering to be that,' said McLure. 'You going to do it for me?'

'I think so,' said Glanville with a chuckle. 'I truly think so, Greg.'

They had entered a small clump of trees, with a narrow track snaking through it. Both men had been so engrossed in their conversation that they had relaxed their guard. They turned a corner. Four dirty and unkempt men in tattered Union uniforms were waiting for them, strung out across the track. Three of them were pointing Sharps Old Reliable carbines at them. The fourth, a man so thin that he resembled a whittled stick, was nursing a single-shot Springfield rifle.

'Howdy,' smirked the carrier of the rifle, revealing blackened and broken teeth. 'We been a-hearing you coming for some time.'

'There was no need to wait for us,' murmured Glanville, sitting very still. 'Mighty neighbourly though.'

'Just wanting to be sociable,' acknowledged the rifle-holder with a broken-toothed snigger.

'You boys on the run?' asked Glanville, taking in the dishevelled state of the four men. They huddled together like desperate rats accustomed to being hunted and resenting the hell out of the fact. Their stench of fear could be sensed even if it could not be smelt. 'Better be on your way. There's a Union railroad gang a couple of

110

miles back.'

'Seen 'em,' spat the leader of the pack vindictively. 'Just a bunch of sod-busters in uniform. Too many of 'em laying track for us to handle though. We thought we'd wait until the odds are better. Looks like we was right. There's four of us and only two of you.'

'True enough.' said McLure stolidly. 'We'll wait until you get another dozen to even things up.'

The leader flushed angrily, while the other three started to surge forward.

'That's big talk for a Johnny Reb,' said the leader, indicating McLure's uniform.

'We're from Slaughter City,' said Glanville, trying to ease the situation. 'Plenty of room for you boys to hole up there. Why don't you ride with us a while?'

'We heard about that place,' said the leader of the deserters bitterly. 'It costs you an arm and a leg just to get past the guards there.'

'Got more brains than I thought,' said

McLure. 'To recognize that you're not even good enough for Slaughter City.'

'Now, Greg,' said Glanville soothingly. He returned his attention to the four men in front of them. 'I could put in a word for you,' he offered.

'Hell, we ain't going to Slaughter City, you know that,' spat one of the deserters in the main group. 'Why don't we just get on with what we had in mind? Shoot 'em down and take what they got.'

His two companions whined their agreement. Their leader shrugged. 'Sorry, partners,' he said with fake regret to the two men ahead of him. 'You can see how it is.'

McLure tensed. The armed gang presented a sorry, defeated sight, but they had their carbines in their hands. By the time he had drawn and downed maybe one of them, the survivors would have filled Glanville and him full of holes. Nevertheless, it was the only option he had.

'He's carrying our poke,' whined Glanville suddenly, pointing fiercely at McLure. 'Take him and leave me.'

The action distracted the deserters for a moment. Their eyes turned on McLure. In the same action Glanville swept his arm round until he was now pointing at the leader of the gang. There was a report and a small black hole appeared in the centre of the renegade's forehead. The man looked faintly surprised and then slipped like a falling sack from the back of his horse. The other three raised their weapons but McLure had already drawn his Colt. In a roar of spitting lead he dropped each of the screaming deserters. They squirmed and lay still. Glanville drew his Smith & Wesson and dismounted, turning each of the four prostrate men with the toe of his boot.

'All dead,' he announced impassively.

'Quite a trick with the sleeve-pistol,' acknowledged McLure. 'Goes with the belly gun you used when I came up against Duvall, and the one I know you keep in your boot. How many more strange places you got pistols hidden? Forget it, I don't want to know. Reckon I owe my life to you.'

'Shucks,' said Glanville nonchalantly. 'I wouldn't have done it if I wasn't good at it. Anyways, I was thinking mainly of my own hide. Come on, if we push our mounts we'll get home in time to eat.'

Without a backward glance at the huddled corpses he spurred his mount ahead. McLure followed him, his head spinning. There was no doubt about it: if Glanville had not shot the first deserter with his sleeve gun he, McLure, would be dead by now. There was no getting away from it: he owed his life to the man he had sworn to kill. He urged his mount forward until he had caught up with his companion. There was something he needed to know.

'This plan of yours,' he said. 'Who are we going to have to take on if we're going to pull it off?'

'Didn't I tell you?' asked Glanville, staring straight ahead, his massive shoulders heaving in a mirthless chuckle. 'We're going to go up against the Union Army.'

TEN

Three days after he had returned from his expedition with Glanville, McLure decided that it was time he made contact with Kelly, the Union agent who was supposed to be waiting up in the hills for him. He rode out of town soon after noon. No one remarked upon his going and he had not seen Glanville since their return, so the town boss could not forbid him to go. It was a chance he had to take.

He reached the wooded foothills in a couple of hours. He found the spot where Pinkerton had bidden him farewell and reined in his horse and waited. Twenty minutes later, a red-haired man emerged cautiously from the bushes. He was lean and wiry, below average height and with a permanent expression of extreme scepticism.

McLure dismounted and tethered his horse to a tree.

'I heard you ten minutes ago,' he told the red-haired man.

'Just making sure you were alone,' sneered Kelly. 'I never have trusted you Southern renegades.'

'I'm not a renegade,' said McLure, surprised that the other man could get under his skin so easily.

'You're working for us, aren't you?' asked Kelly. He laughed bitterly. 'Oh, I see. Pinkerton's been giving you his spiel about one united nation in the future. If you believe that you'll believe anything. Once this war is won we're going to squeeze the juice out of you like Californian oranges.'

There was more in the same vein but McLure had stopped listening. When Kelly paused to draw breath he interrupted curtly, 'I've no cause to love you either, but I've got news for you to take to Pinkerton, so listen up.'

The name of the spymaster was enough to

cut Kelly short. The Union agent listened in silence as McLure gave him an account of all that had happened since he had arrived in Slaughter City.

'Right,' he said ungraciously when McLure had finished. 'I'll see that my report goes to Mr Pinkerton. Wouldn't count too much on him reading it though. He's got more important things to do. So have I.'

'I want you to stay here,' McLure told him sharply. 'I may need help.'

'You surely may,' jeered the Union man. 'What have you done so far, eh? You could have gunned down Glanville and ridden to hell and on by now.'

'I want to find out what he's planning,' said McLure. 'It might be important.'

'Nothing that happens in that one-horse shanty-town is important. You're just cosying up to Glanville in case there's some return in it for you.'

'There's something else,' said McLure, ignoring the insult. 'The deputy I shot, did you see from here if the wagon carrying him went past to Maddox?'

Kelly shrugged indifferently 'A wagon went past all right,' he conceded grudgingly. 'It was going in the general direction of Maddox. I couldn't see the shot deputy in the back, but there was three up on the box. Two men and a woman.' He stopped, squinting shrewdly at McLure. 'Something wrong?'

'No,' said McLure evasively. 'I'd better be getting back.'

'Give me ten minutes' start,' said Kelly, disappearing among the bushes.

McLure waited for ten minutes and then mounted his horse and started riding back towards Slautara. Kelly had given him plenty to think about. It was obvious from the agent's manner that no matter how much he helped the Union cause in Slaughter City, the victorious Union forces would have little time for any Southerner. He was just someone to be used and then discarded. Perhaps he had better start making his own long-term plans.

But something else that Kelly had said worried him much more. The agent had informed him that there had been two men and a woman on the board of the covered wagon leaving Slaughter City on the night of the shooting. But apart from Wiley, who had been lying seriously injured in the back, only Kearns and Nora had driven out.

Who was the other man?

ELEVEN

'There's been a shooting at the Golden Nugget,' said one of the deputies tersely, putting his head round the door of McLure's office. 'One wounded, the other blowing a lot of steam.'

'How come he had a pistol?' demanded McLure, rising and buckling on his gunbelt before following the deputy down the crowded morning street in the direction of the saloon. 'You're supposed to search everybody.'

'Hell, Greg, you know what it's been like this last week,' protested the aggrieved deputy. 'We've had more men drifting into the town than we can cope with.'

The man was right, thought McLure. For the past seven days, ever since he had returned from his meeting with Kelly, he and his deputies had been stretched to their limits trying to maintain order among the ever increasing number of hard-cases demanding shelter in the town. The newcomers had brought with them conflicting rumours that the war was in its last days. Some even said that General Lee's troops defending Richmond had been driven back and that the Confederate military leader had already surrendered to Grant before riding sadly back to his Virginia plantation.

Whatever the truth of the stories, the plains approaching Slautara were infested with packs of desperate men like the ones McLure and Glanville had encountered on their recent ride back to the town – deserters, escaped slaves, outlaws all living off the land, robbing and pillaging. McLure and his deputies still admitted only those who could pay for their stay and were prepared to give up their sidearms, but they were now desperately outnumbered by the renegades demanding shelter. It was obvious to the newcomers that law and order was on the verge of breaking down. Some of them, he knew, were smuggling pistols into the town and there was nothing that he could do about it. The shooting just reported in the saloon was a case in point.

Glanville had been no help at all when the marshal's worries had been conveyed to him. The town boss had dismissed Mc-Lure's problems airily. 'Just keep the lid on the kettle a little longer, Greg,' the man had begged. 'Buy me a little more time and then I'll be able to cut you in on the sweetest deal you ever got near. Trust me.'

Glanville certainly was playing his cards close to his vest again. He rode out of town most mornings and did not appear again until shortly before sundown. He was keeping an eye on something. McLure wondered whether the repair of the railroad track they had witnessed together had anything to do with it. For the hundredth time he wondered why he did not just shoot Glanville out of hand and have done with it. He could call the town boss out, cut him down in a hail of lead and be out of the town before anyone could do anything about it.

Only there was a fresh problem. With the recent influx of outlaws and renegades the town was close to anarchy. With the town boss dead and the marshal fled, the bandits would cut down any deputies who tried to face them and simply take over the town. That meant that the ordinary citizens would be robbed and killed to just the same shameful degree as Bloody Bill Anderson had displayed at Centralia. McLure had no time for the citizens who had turned a blind eye to the presence of the renegades and had eagerly accepted their money, but he knew that he could not ride away and leave them to the slaughter that would surely follow if neither he nor Glanville were left to control the town. There was also the fact that after the incident with the band of deserters outside the town he owed Glanville his life, but he did not want to think about that.

He shouldered his way in through the batwing doors of the Golden Nugget. There was a crowd around a man lying bleeding on the floor. Another man, truculent and unshaven, was standing with his back to the wall, a Colt in his hand. Half-a-dozen deputies had fanned out uneasily in front of him, each unwilling to make the first move.

'What happened?' McLure asked the sweating bartender. 'Poker game,' answered the nervous bar-dog. He indicated the man with the Colt. 'Big Hank accused Joe of cheating. Joe pulled a knife, and Hank drew on him and plugged him.'

McLure nodded. He walked over to the ring of deputies. At the sight of the marshal the big man raised his Colt. The deputies shuffled back. It was a sign of the break-down in control that they had allowed Hank to survive this long, thought McLure. The six of them could have brought the big man down easily enough, but they had probably been afraid of the reaction of the crowd if they had done so.

'All right, Hank,' he said wearily. 'Give me your Colt and come to the calaboose with me.'

'I ain't going nowhere,' said the big man defiantly. 'Joe had an ace up his sleeve.' He turned to the others. 'Ain't that right?' he demanded loudly.

There were nods and murmurs of agreement from the crowd. Plainly the wounded man had few supporters among them. Or perhaps they were just plain scared of Hank. McLure weighed up the odds. Hank already had his pistol drawn. He would get off at least one shot before he could be nailed. That one shot might prove to be fatal.

'You leave Joe be,' said Hank wildly. 'He asked for all he got. Let him bleed right there by the spittoons.'

'Got to take you in, Hank,' said McLure doggedly, aware that his throat was as dry as a pebble in a desert.

'Try it,' warned the other man, 'and you've bought a one-way ticket to Boot Hill.'

McLure took a pace forward. Hank raised

his pistol with shaking hands and levelled it at the marshal. McLure's heart was pounding but he forced himself to take a second pace forward. He was still too far away to jump the other man. Hank growled. His finger began to curl on the trigger.

'Hold it right there, Hank,' said a voice from behind the bar. All eyes swivelled in the direction of the voice. Glanville was standing behind the counter. He was levelling a shotgun at Hank.

'You've had your fun,' said the town boss. 'Now throw down your pistol before I drop you like a bad habit.'

Hank's attention flashed wildly from McLure to Glanville and then back to the marshal again. The man's face was streaked with sweat.

'My pistol's drawn,' he blustered. 'I could still gun the marshal before you could get your shot off.'

'You sure could,' said Glanville with apparent unconcern. 'Wouldn't stop me cutting you in half straight afterwards though. Think about it, Hank. I can always get me another marshal; you've just got the one life, ornery as it is.' His voice hardened. 'I've had enough of playing games, son. I'm going to count to three and then let her rip.'

The crowd inside the saloon scattered and men threw themselves without shame to the floor at the words. Only McLure and Hank were left standing in the centre of the room. Hank's face was white beneath the rivulets of perspiration coursing down it. Unemotionally Glanville raised his bulky shotgun. McLure tensed himself for the shot which surely would come from Hank. The poker player threw one last desperate glance around the saloon. The panic-stricken reactions of the other drinkers cowering behind the tables and chairs were enough to convince him that the town boss's intentions were as deadly as death itself. He allowed his pistol to fall to the ground. An audible sigh of relief passed like a spring breeze round the crowded saloon. McLure stooped and picked up the other man's weapon.

'Take him to the lock-up,' he ordered the deputies.

He watched as his assistants hustled their prisoner out. Glanville lifted the bar-flap and walked over to join him.

'Thanks,' said McLure tonelessly. 'That's the second time you've saved my life.'

'I've told you,' grinned Glanville. 'I need you, Greg. Why else would I bother? Let's take a walk.'

The town boss pushed open the doors and they started walking down the main street.

'I rode to the rail-head at Fork Springs today,' he announced suddenly.

'Oh yes, and why would you do that?' asked McLure, trying to sound casual.

'I wanted to see just how far they'd got with repairing the stretch of railroad. They've just about finished it. That means we can get on with my plan tomorrow. Be ready to ride out with me after breakfast. Bring enough supplies for a couple of days. And no, I'm not going to tell you what it is.

Time enough for that.'

Before McLure could ask any questions, a shout from one of the deputies made them both turn. The deputy was escorting a horse and its rider down the main street. Both the mount and the dust-covered cowpoke, a lean, sun-wrinkled man with a drooping moustache, were showing signs of many hours of recent hard riding.

'This man's from Maddox City,' explained the deputy 'Says he's got a message from Kearns for you.'

'How's Wiley?' burst out McLure before Glanville could reply. 'That the guy with the gunshot wound?' asked the rider without interest. 'They operated on him at the hospital. It was touch-and-go but the docs think he should pull through. Kearns says he and the nurse will stay with him for a while and come back to Slaughter City in ten days or so.'

McLure experienced a wave of relief. Even Glanville showed some signs of satisfaction. 'Thanks, pardner,' he told the cowpoke. The town boss patted his pockets. 'I don't have much money on me. Come with me to the hotel and I'll give you something for your trouble and arrange for you to eat and rest up. We'll drop your mount off at the livery stables on the way.'

Glanville walked away, leading the horse by the bridle. He turned back briefly to look at McLure.

'Do me a favour, Greg,' he begged. 'Try to keep out of trouble until tomorrow morning, huh?'

TWELVE

They rode out shortly before sun-up the following morning. McLure had packed his few belongings into his saddle-bags. Glanville was carrying his necessities for the journey in several gunny sacks attached to the pommel of his saddle. For his part, McLure was taking out of the town only his Colt and Winchester and the few dollars he had earned as marshal over the past few weeks. Both men were carrying their bedrolls across their saddles.

They rode in silence for several hours across the short-grass plain and up into the ever-ascending, thickly forested foothills. They moved with caution among the cedars and cottonwoods. They could hear others moving among the undergrowth, and every so often they caught glimpses of packs of tattered, hungry-looking renegades, clad in rags of uniforms, moving among the trees. Most were on foot and the few pitiable horses that were to be seen were so emaciated that their ribs strained against their skins like the staves of broken barrels. Many of the men were missing an arm or a leg. Most had grimy bloodstained bandages rotting like extra peeling skins. They all looked like old men who had seen too much and as a result had been transmuted into half-wolves.

'Bet those boys never thought they'd be praying to eat hardtack and pork again,' said Glanville. 'They reckoned they'd take to desertion like a frog to a pond.'

'It'll get worse than this,' predicted McLure after they had made a detour through the trees to skirt one particularly large party of deserters. 'When the war does end, they'll be sending the Union soldier-boys home. There'll be thousands of 'em covering the countryside, and some of 'em won't be too particular how they pick up spending money on the way.'

'Not just yet,' said Glanville smugly. 'Those bluebellies won't be going anywhere for a while, believe me.'

The big man was moving his horse with a certainty that indicated that he knew where he was going and that he wanted to be there within a certain time-limit. McLure contented himself with cantering a few yards behind the town boss. Again and again the thought crossed his mind that this would be as good a time as any to have it out with Glanville and gun him down for deserting at Shiloh and exposing the surviving Confederates to the fatal Union charge. Something told McLure that the time had not yet come. He wanted to know just what the other man's plans were.

By early evening they were riding along a high, flat-topped ridge with a dense dusting of thickly entwined hardwood trees providing sources of shelter and concealment along the way. Glanville increased his pace and entered the trees, swaying in his saddle to avoid the swinging branches. McLure dug his heels into the flanks of his mount and went after the town boss. The foliage almost blotted out the sun and he had to squint to accustom his eyes to the gloom. A covered wagon was waiting close to four hobbled mules and two horses grazing placidly in a clearing. Two unshaven men and a woman were drinking coffee by a camp-fire. McLure reined in his horse, scarcely able to believe the evidence of his eyes. The woman was Nora Wright and one of her companions was Kearns, the young deputy Glanville had sent with her to Maddox City.

It was the second man who was the recipient of McLure's full attention. Calmly sipping his coffee and grinning up at him was Seb Wiley, the chief deputy he had gunned down in the livery stables.

THIRTEEN

'Don't look so startled, Greg,' chuckled Glanville. 'Old Wiley here ain't buzzard-bait just yet.'

Ten minutes had passed since Glanville and McLure had ridden into the camp. They were sitting round the fire with the others, drinking coffee poured for them by a blank-faced Nora. It looked as if the others had been here for some time. A deer had been killed and hung to dry on a juniper.

'Somebody going to tell me what's going on?' asked McLure, making no effort to conceal his anger at being duped. Wiley must have been the second man on the box of the wagon reported by Kelly. 'What's a supposedly badly injured man doing a' setting here as large as life and twice as ugly?'

The three other men laughed. No expression crossed Nora's face. She sat apart from the others, half-turned away, nursing her cup of coffee.

'Sorry I had to pull this one on you, Greg,' said Glanville contritely 'It was necessary though. You see, I had to get my three best men out of Slaughter City to help me with a job. Only everybody knew I had this rule that no deputy was ever allowed out of Slautara. So how was I to get Wiley and Kearns away from town in advance to wait for us here?'

'You fixed the shooting,' McLure told him slowly, comprehending. 'You arranged the attack on me and fixed Wiley up in advance covered in goat's blood or something, so that when we found him I would take it that I'd shot him.'

'Don't think it was easy,' said Wiley with feeling, reaching forward to refill his cup. 'When you started firing back at me in the dark some of the shots as near as damn-it took my head off.'

'So that's why you wouldn't let me go too near Wiley in the barn,' McLure said to a grinning Glanville. 'You knew I'd spot the fake blood.' He swung round on Nora. She did not meet his gaze. 'And you were in on it too. You knew before you even got to the stables that you would find Wiley pretending to be wounded.'

'I knew nobody would question the town nurse,' said Glanville complacently. 'Can't say that Nora exactly liked the idea, or even knew what it was all about, but she didn't have much choice, not if she wanted to be allowed to stay in Slautara.'

'All right,' conceded McLure reluctantly. 'I can see the point in getting Wiley and Kearns away. But why didn't you let me in on it? Why did you leave me to think that I'd hurt Wiley?'

'Sorry about that, Greg,' said Glanville. 'But you're sometimes a tad too bright for your own good. If I had let you in on the plan you would have started wondering about what I had in store. Might even have made a guess at it too. No, you were better off thinking that you'd shot Wiley down. It kept your mind off other things.'

'Thanks very much,' said McLure bitterly. 'So are you going to tell me now?'

Glanville shook his head. 'Not none of you,' he said with finality. 'Tomorrow sun-up will be time enough for all of you to know.' He turned to Wiley. 'Has there been any trouble since you arrived?'

'None,' answered the grizzled deputy. 'Most of the gangs are drifting east. Easier pickings there. No one left to rob this side of the mountain ridge except the bluecoats at Fort Henry, and they ain't stupid enough to pick on hard-nosed soldier-boys. No one's going to find us here unless they're looking for us deliberate-like.'

'There's a stream running down to the valley just a hundred yards away,' added Kearns. 'It's as good a place to pitch camp as any.'

Glanville sipped his coffee complacently. 'I know all that,' he boasted. 'I first scouted the place a couple of years ago. Soon after I first came to Slautara. Hell, the only reason I came to the town was because it was near here and I knew that one day I would be able to pull off a job that would make me rich.'

'Don't you mean make *us* rich?' asked Wiley quietly, but with an unmistakable edge to his tone.

Glanville stared at him coldly for a moment and then laughed. 'There's pickings for us all here, don't worry about that,' he said dismissively. 'I've been planning it long enough. Just remember, without me you boys would be wading through a mire of bull-wallow.'

'So maybe you'd like to let me in on the secret?' suggested McLure.

Glanville shook his head. 'Tomorrow,' he promised. 'It's all coming off tomorrow, that's all you need to know. I'm going to need the three of you. Just do as you're told and we'll come out of this with enough to set us up for the rest of our lives. Until then, we'll cook something to eat and get an early night. If you want to help, Greg, you can grain our horses and take 'em to drink at the stream over through the trees there.'

Wiley started to skin the deer preparatory to slicing the meat into strips, while Kearns notched two greenwood sticks and stuck them in the ground on either side of the flames before placing a third branch horizontally between the two uprights, upon which to dangle and cook the meat. Glanville took bread wrapped in a square of muslin from his saddle-bag. McLure fed the two horses and then took them through the trees towards the water as the other men and Nora started preparing the evening meal. He could sense that matters were coming to a head. McLure arrived at a decision. He would wait until Glanville had showed him what he had in his mind and then he would dispose of the town boss, as he had intended all along.

He sat on the bank of the stream with his back against a sapling and looked on idly as the two hobbled horses drank. Pines and evergreen ashes twisted and tortured with undergrowth were so closely packed together that he could hear no sounds coming from the camp-site behind him in the hollow a hundred yards away. A scattering of gravel beach fringed the water, while a swaying arrow of willows ran out over a smooth sandbar. He rose and moved farther upstream to refill his water bottle. As he did so he heard the snap of a twig coming from among the trees running down to the waterside. He drew his Colt. Nora Wright stepped out of the trees. She placed a finger to her lips.

'Keep your voice down,' she warned. 'They sent me out to fetch kindling for the fire. I think Glanville wanted to talk to the other two. I can't stay long.' She hesitated and then burst out impulsively, 'I want your help, Greg.'

'They been treating you right?' asked McLure softly. 'They ain't–'

'No, nothing like that. Wiley and Kearns

might have fancied taking me, but they had strict orders from Glanville that I was to be left alone, and they're both scared of him.' She tried to restrain a shiver. 'I reckon Glanville's got his own plans for me when all this is over.'

'How much are you in on this?' McLure wanted to know badly. 'You were with Duvall. Does that mean that you and Glanville–?'

'Pete Duvall was slime,' said the woman calmly. 'I was with him because I had to have a protector if I wanted to stop in Slautara. I was mad at you when you killed him because I thought I would get thrown out to take my chances again.'

'I didn't want to kill Duvall,' McLure told her sincerely. 'It was self-defence.'

'I didn't care that he was dead,' the girl said steadily. 'I was glad even. And to answer your question, I'm nothing to Glanville. I don't know what he's got in his crooked mind and I don't want to. I'm just looking to keep alive.' The girl took a step back.

Suddenly she looked young and vulnerable. She dropped her eyes. 'I wanted you to know that, Marshal.'

'I'll do my best to look after you,' McLure promised, touched by the appeal. The girl's words had lifted a weight from his mind, one that had been there ever since he had first met her at the surgery and Glanville had told her that he was Duvall's killer.

Nora nodded and tried to smile. 'I know you will,' she whispered, and turned to disappear among the trees.

McLure's mind was working busily as he collected the two horses. He did not know whether to be pleased or dismayed by the girl's revelation that she was only an innocent bystander. On the one hand he was warmed to discover that she had no part in Glanville's plans.

On the other, it meant that he now had to look after her as well as himself.

FOURTEEN

They were all up as the sun began to edge over the horizon the following morning. The men had each taken a two-hour shift on guard, keeping the fire replenished. Nora, who had been sleeping in the wagon, fixed a breakfast of bacon and the corn porridge known as atole over the fire. Kearns made the bellywash he called coffee. As the young woman washed up, Kearns and Wiley hitched the draw mules to the wagon.

'You and me will ride ahead,' Glanville told McLure. 'The other two know where to bring the wagon.'

'What about Nora?' asked McLure, trying to appear casual as he buckled on his gunbelt.

Glanville looked at him shrewdly. 'Don't worry,' he said, walking towards his horse.

'She'll travel in the wagon. No harm will come to her, I give you my word on it.'

The pair of them rode out of the camp and along a track sloping down towards the foothills. After an hour, Glanville stopped amid an outer ring of trees in a valley between two hills.

'There you are,' he indicated. 'Sweet as a nut, ain't it?'

McLure followed the town boss's gaze. A railroad track ran like a twisting iron snake through the valley and then eased its way up the hill before descending on the far side.

'All the way from Maddox City to the end of the line we saw being repaired a couple of weeks ago,' Glanville said expansively. 'Ain't she a beaut?'

'If you like railroads,' agreed McLure cautiously.

'Love 'em,' said Glanville with enthusiasm. 'Used to work on the Chicago and Galena line before the war. Engineer laying line. Always planned to use my expertise on a job like this one day. Never thought it would come like this though. Not until I drifted into Slaughter City and kind of took it over.'

'You're going to hold up a train,' guessed McLure. It should have been obvious sooner. That ride they had taken to observe the progress of relaying the line ought to have alerted him as to what was being planned.

'Not any train,' Glanville reproved him. 'The payroll caboose to Fort Henry. It's due in three hours. It will be loaded with wages for the soldier-boys.'

'And guarded by them same soldier-boys too,' warned McLure.

Glanville waved away his doubts. 'Damn me if you ain't as balky as a mule, Greg. We got a hole card. They haven't been in action for almost a year and they know the war's close to over. There won't be more than a dozen on board and the last thing they'll be expecting is trouble. When the train reaches the end of the line they'll unload the wages on to wagons and carry them the last ten miles to the fort. If they're expecting any trouble it will be on that last leg. That's why the train's being met by another thirty mounted troops. We'll hit 'em so hard here before they're expecting it they'll think they're back at Bull Run and start looking for badger-holes to crawl into.'

'How do you know it'll be coming today?' asked McLure.

'I told you, I've been planning this for years.' There was a maniacal glint in Glanville's eyes and his cheeks were flushed with excitement. 'One last big job and we'll high-tail it away and live high off the hog for the rest of our lives. I've watched a dozen wage trains come along this stretch over the last year and I know everything about 'em. Slim Callaway, the cowpoke who rode into Slautara yesterday, didn't have any news about Wiley and the hospital. He was just confirming that the train was running to schedule today.'

'Nice idea,' McLure forced himself to concede. 'But haven't you forgotten one thing?

Those wages will be in gold coins. Even if we pull off the hold-up, we won't be able to carry too many cases away in the wagon without they go through the floor.'

'That's just where you're wrong, Greg my boy,' laughed Glanville condescendingly. 'Haven't you heard? The bluebellies haven't paid their soldier-boys in gold for the last year. They've been issuing paper money. Scrip, they call it. That's what will be on the train. Light-weighing paper money. I figure we can carry off a hundred thousand dollars without breaking into a sweat. And in the North that paper money will buy exactly the same as gold.' He took a watch from his pocket and consulted it. 'Wiley and Kearns should be here with the wagon inside an hour. We'll just wait here for them.'

The two deputies arrived within forty-five minutes. They concealed the wagon among the trees and left the mules hitched to the shafts. Wiley detached one of the horses from its leadrope and fetched a saddle from the wagon, securing it into place on the horse's back. As he did so, McLure caught a brief glimpse of Nora moving about inside the wagon. Glanville greeted the newcomers with a nod.

'Did you cut them trees down like I told you while you were waiting during the week?' he asked.

'All done for,' answered Wiley, indicating a pile of timber half obscured under a covering of leaves in a clearing. 'As soon as the train has gone past, Kearns'll pile 'em on the track.'

'Good,' said Glanville. 'Kearns, you wait here with the woman until you see the engine. McLure and Wiley, you ride with me.'

Glanville walked over to the wagon and said something in an undertone to Nora. She stooped and picked up a large tub and a long-handled miner's hammer, which she handed down to the town boss. Glanville mounted his horse, balancing the wooden container before him on the pommel and swinging the hammer in the hand not occupied with the reins. McLure and Wiley climbed into their saddles. McLure noticed that the senior deputy had two of the new Henry sixteen-shot repeaters thrust into carriers dangling before his knees and that he was cramming two tins each containing 200 shells into his saddle-bags.

Glanville led them up the slope, following the line of railroad track. A heavy dusting of trees extended almost to the iron rails. The town boss had chosen his spot carefully. No one on the train would be able to see marauders in the woods, even if they were lurking only a few yards away. McLure experienced the familiar tingling sensation in his body that he had always felt before going into battle. It had been a long time, he thought. For a moment he worried about accompanying Glanville on his attack, but he dismissed the thought. They were going up against Union soldiers, as he had done a dozen times before his capture. It was just another campaign. He would deal with Glanville as soon as it was over.

At a spot chosen by Glanville close to the top of the hill, the three men dismounted and tethered their mounts to trees. At once Wiley dropped behind the shelter of a large rock overlooking the line, at the same time checking his rifles and then carefully placing a box of ammunition at his side. Glanville indicated to McLure.

'Give me a hand on the track,' he said.

They emerged from the trees on foot and approached the iron line. Glanville carried the tub. He wrenched off the lid to reveal that it was full of thick axle-grease. He plunged his hands up to his elbow in the semi-liquid mess and started greasing the railroad line, applying a thick coating.

'You take the other side,' he ordered McLure. 'Get as much of this stuff on the rail as you can for twenty yards.'

McLure hurried to obey, keeping pace with the other man in applying great gobbets of grease. When they had finished Glanville scrutinized the now glistening lines with satisfaction.

'Always worked before when I tried it,' he said, half to himself. 'No reason why it shouldn't now. Come on, it's time we were back in the trees.'

They retrieved their position next to Wiley behind the rock and waited. Thirty minutes dragged like so many hours. Then they heard the distant chug of an engine. Glanville tensed. 'You stay here,' he ordered McLure in an undertone. 'Wiley, I'm depending on you to keep them bluebellies pinned down while I uncouple the boxcar and for as long as you can after. Greg, as soon as you see the car running back down the hill, ride back down behind it with me.'

The wood-burning locomotive came steaming round the corner, steam billowing from its chimney-shaped funnel, and laboriously began to climb the hill towards them. There were only two boxcars attached to the locomotive. McLure could see the engineer and the fireman moving in the cab.

'They reckon any attack will take the form of an ambush,' whispered Glanville, his eyes fixed intently on the advancing train. 'They've got most of the troops in the first box-car, so that they can fire out if anyone tries to attack, while the train gathers speed. The money's in the second car with no windows, together with four soldiers at most.'

It made sense, thought McLure. The troops and their officers would be conditioned to full-scale military attacks and were prepared to repel them. Knowing Glanville as he did, and taking into account the amount of grease smeared so liberally on the length of track before them, he guessed that Glanville had something altogether sneakier in mind.

'Wish me luck,' said Glanville suddenly, and started crawling out of the trees towards the line, dragging the large hammer with him. He waited until the train was almost opposite him. The wheels of the locomotive started to spin helplessly on the greased rails. The train slowed and then, as the wheels failed to get any purchase on the line, started to slide backwards. At once the driver applied the brakes, bringing the train to a shuddering halt. The engineer and the fireman stared down at the line ahead of them. Glanville rose and raced forward to the front of the last box-car. Swinging his hammer vigorously he brought it down again and again on the iron pin and link which secured the coupling linking the car to the remainder of the train. At first the pin did not move, but several more blows with the hammer drove it out of the link. Unencumbered, the box-car started rolling back down the line towards the foot of the hill, increasing its speed as it gathered momentum. The perspiring Glanville dropped the hammer and sprinted back for the safety of the trees.

The engineer and fireman shouted angrily and leapt down from the footplate to gather soil and dust to strew over the greased line. As they did so Wiley opened fire with his rifle from behind the rock. The bullets spat like angry hornets on the iron line, close to the feet of the two men. At once the engineer and the fireman abandoned their task and jumped back up into the cab, cowering behind the open boiler door.

'Come on!' Glanville shouted to McLure, leaping on to his horse. McLure obeyed. As he spurred his mount through the trees after the other man, he looked over his shoulder at the train. The soldiers who had occupied the remaining box-car had slid the door open. However, a volley of accurate shots from Wiley smashed into the open car. Immediately, the flustered troops drew the door shut again and contented themselves with yelling angrily and directing a volley of aimless rounds into the trees through slits in the side of the car.

'They think they're being ambushed!' shouted Glanville as McLure caught up with him. 'With a load of luck Wiley should be able to keep 'em pinned down for twenty minutes or so. They don't have horses, so we could get a few of those money boxes loaded and away!'

When they reached the bottom of the hill McLure saw why Kearns and Wiley had assembled the cache of sawn timber. After they had left him to ride up the slope the deputy had obviously piled the logs high across the track, keeping them in place with several thick vertical struts of wood. The runaway box-car had careered into the obstacle at full tilt and had come off the track. It was lying on its side, one of the doors smashed open and its wheels still spinning helplessly, like a gigantic discarded toy.

The four occupants of the car had not fared well in the smash. Two of them lay crumpled and groaning on the floor. The other two soldiers had been flung clear and were lying inert and face downwards on the track. Kearns had collected their rifles and side-arms and piled them under a tree. He was in the process of dragging heavy boxes from the wreck along the ground to the waiting covered wagon.

Glanville and McLure dismounted and helped the deputy in his task, loading the chests into the wagon, watched by an impassive Nora. From further up the hill they could hear the ragged and discordant rattle of rifle-fire as Wiley continued to pin down the troops in the other box-car. He was discharging his two weapons so rapidly that the soldiers returning his fire blindly must have thought that they had been ambushed by a gang of four or five.

'That's enough,' said Glanville sharply, after they had heaved ten of the large boxes of paper money into the wagon.

'There's another dozen boxes left in the train,' protested Kearns.

'I've got this worked out,' said Glanville sharply. 'We've got to get a good start on the bluebellies and give Wiley time to disengage and follow us. You drive the wagon. Me and McLure will ride alongside.'

As the town boss issued his orders, McLure suddenly caught the briefest of glimpses of light among the trees, as if a shaft of sunlight penetrating the branches had suddenly been deflected. While Kearns and Glanville prepared to move off watched by Nora, McLure drifted casually into the forest. Once he was among the trees he drew his Colt. Stealthily he moved forward, taking a roundabout route. Crouched behind a tree, their carbines trained on the covered wagon were three Union troops, a sergeant and two young privates.

McLure cursed beneath his breath. Despite all Wiley's efforts, this group must have got out of the box-car at the top of the slope and made its way down to see what had happened to the other car. If one of the Union troops had not grown careless as they advanced through the trees they would have been able to shoot the three of them down as they finished loading the wagon.

'Hold it right there, boys,' said McLure.

The three startled men squirmed round on their bellies. When they saw the Colt pointing at them the two privates dropped their weapons fast. The sergeant, a much older man, clung on to his for a second and then put it down with reluctance.

'How the hell did you know we was here?' he asked, rising to his feet.

'Saw the sunlight coming off a barrel of a rifle,' McLure told him.

The sergeant directed a withering glare at his two young charges. 'I told you to keep them carbines a-covered,' he rasped.

'Like to stop chatting here to you all day, Sergeant, but I got work to do,' said McLure. 'Would you Union boys kindly walk out of the trees in the direction of the rail track?'

Glanville and Kearns stopped work in amazement when McLure emerged from the trees with his three prisoners stumbling before him.

'Dammit, Greg!' exclaimed Glanville in delight, 'I knew you'd come in useful one day.'

'Southern scum!' spat the sergeant, gazing up through misting eyes at the remnants of McLure's Confederate grey uniform. 'Well, trust you to be too little and too late.'

'What you talking about, Sergeant?' asked McLure.

'Never mind socializing with 'em!' exploded Glanville. 'Kill the three of 'em and let's be off.'

'Can't do that,' said McLure. 'They're prisoners of war.'

'You gone loco?' demanded the sergeant. 'There ain't no war. Lee surrendered three days ago.'

'Is that true?' demanded McLure, whirling round on Glanville.

'Didn't I tell you?' asked Glanville casually. 'Must have plain slipped my mind. I'm afraid that wasn't no military operation you just took part in, just a plain old-fashioned hold-up. For which you will be hanged if we are caught.' He indicated the three Union soldiers. 'So, shoot 'em down.'

'Still can't do that,' said McLure steadily. He looked at Kearns. 'Get some rope from the wagon and tie the three of 'em to trees.'

'The hell I will,' said Kearns indignantly.

Without appearing to take aim McLure let

163

off a shot. It spat into the dust only inches from Kearn's feet. Kearn backed off to the wagon.

'Don't go inside where I can't see you,' McLure warned him. 'Get Nora to hand you down three lengths of rope and then tie these soldier-boys up.'

Covered by the Colt, Kearns did as he was asked. When he had finished binding the three men McLure holstered his Colt.

'All right, we can go now,' he said.

'You take a lot on yourself, Greg,' said Glanville, suffused with anger. 'You ever pull a gun on me again and you'd better be ready to use it.'

'And you've been playing me for a fool,' retorted McLure. 'Reckon we've both got a mite to say to each other on our trip back.'

Kearns took his place on the box of the wagon. McLure and Glanville mounted. As he gentled his horse round by the tailgate McLure looked up at Nora, expecting to find that she, at least, would approve of what had happened to the soldiers. Instead she was looking at him with undisguised anger.

'You should have killed the three of them,' she hissed. 'I would have!'

FIFTEEN

They travelled along the forest track as fast as the team could be urged for an hour before Wiley caught up with them, his horse's flanks sweating with the effort of the ride. With a triumphant grin the chief deputy swung his horse in alongside Glanville.

'How were things back at the track?' asked the town boss, not slackening his pace.

'Lively,' said Wiley laconically. 'I winged about four of 'em. Two or three got away towards the end though and headed down the track towards you.'

'Don't worry, Greg here dealt with 'em real tidy,' chuckled the town boss. 'He can shoot nearly as good as you, Wiley.'

'Are the bluebellies coming after us?' asked Kearns anxiously from his place on the box of the wagon. Nora was somewhere inside the vehicle.

Wiley shook his head. 'Not after that turkey shoot. They didn't have mounts,' he answered. 'Most of 'em were tending their wounded. By the time they get a message to the soldier-boys awaiting at the railhead, we'll be back in Slaughter City.'

'Then what?' asked McLure. He had overcome his anger at being duped by Glanville and knew that he would have to make some sort of move before they reached Slautara. 'The Union won't take this lying down. They'll send a real force in against us. And you've already pulled the explosives trick. They'll be watching out for it this time. They'll take the town for certain sure.'

''Course they will,' agreed Glanville. 'But not straight away, and we won't be there when they do. I told you, I've had years to plan this. I've found a back way out of Slautara through the hills. Won't be easy, but if we make it, those greenbacks'll set us up for life.' He reined in his horse suddenly

168

and drew his Colt, levelling it at McLure. 'All except for you, Greg, I'm afraid,' he said with mild regret. 'I'm afraid this is the end of the line for you, partner!'

'What are you talking about?' asked McLure, a hollow feeling in the pit of his stomach. He should have known better than to let his concentration wander, but he had been concerned about attacking the Union train while he was no longer a soldier. Kearns had reined in the wagon and was scrambling down, pointing a carbine at him. Similarly, with a wolfish grin Wiley had also drawn his revolver.

'Grieves me to say this,' smirked Glanville, 'but you were always expendable, Greg. Me and Wiley and Kearns decided that we'd take you along because an extra gunman would be useful. Afraid we never had any intention of cutting you in though.'

Wiley and Kearns laughed coarsely. McLure had to clench his fists to quell his fury. It had all been a trap! All that he had ever meant to Glanville was as an extra gunman in case matters got tricky. Well, it looked as if he was going to pay with his life for his lack of attention to what should have been his duty.

'Sorry, Greg,' shrugged Glanville, 'but you were always a mite too sharp for me. I prefer to work with pack-mules like Kearns and Wiley.'

He raised his Colt. There was a sudden thunder of wheels and the grunts of surprised mules being urged forward. Instinctively Glanville, Wiley and Kearns looked in the direction of the covered wagon. Nora was sitting on the box, the reins in her hands, urging the vehicle along the track away from them.

'She's getting away with the money!' shouted a startled Kearns, loosing off a snap shot at the departing covered wagon. Glanville and Wiley jerked their attention back to McLure in alarm, but the marshal had already cleared leather with his Colt. He cut down Wiley and Kearns with his first two shots. Glanville managed to get off one shot in return, but the noise of the gunfire had startled his mount, which reared and unsettled its rider. Glanville's shot was buried harmlessly among the trees. McLure fired again in almost the same instant. His bullet caught Glanville in the arm, sending out a gusher of blood and forcing the town boss to cry out in pain and drop his revolver. McLure fired again, but with an oath Glanville reared his horse round and hurtled it into the trees, away from the track. McLure fired in the direction of the noise but he knew that Glanville had got away. He holstered his Colt and went over to examine the two bodies. Wiley was dead, shot through the forehead, but although Kearns had taken a bullet in the chest he was still alive, breathing only shallowly. McLure heard footsteps and looked up. Nora was walking back to him along the track.

'Thanks for distracting them,' he said. 'I thought I was a gonner.'

Nora knelt to examine the two bodies. 'I

didn't do it for you,' she said abstractedly. 'I just thought there was more to you than there was to the other three, and I need help with my mission.' She stood up again. 'Do you think Glanville will come back?'

'I doubt it,' said McLure. 'He dropped his Colt. We'll be out of the trees in ten minutes. If he tries to approach us as we cross open country we'll be able to see him a mile away.'

'Help me get Kearns back into the wagon,' said the girl. 'There's not much I can do for him, but he'll be slightly better off in Slaughter City than dying here on the trail.'

With a considerable effort, McLure and Nora lifted the injured and unconscious deputy over the tailgate of the wagon and made him as comfortable as they could on a pile of feed sacks among the payroll chests. Nora poured disinfectant over the gaping wound and then rubbed sulfa salve over it from the medicine box in the wagon. When she had finished, McLure held up the injured man while Nora wound bandages around his chest. Finally she gave the semi-conscious deputy laudanum to dull the pain. 'Best I can do for now,' she said. 'We'd better make for Slaughter City.'

McLure wondered if he would ever understand her. An hour ago she had been condemning him for sparing the lives of the three Union soldiers. Now no one could have treated the wounded Kearns more tenderly or with such care. He decided that Nora was a complex woman.

'I'll bury Wiley before we leave,' he offered, picking up a spade.

'Only if you want the Union troops catching up with us before we can get away,' said Nora forcefully.

McLure took her point and dropped the spade. They took their places on the box and started the frightened horses back along the track towards Slautara. McLure cast a sideways look at Nora. She looked as composed as if she was sitting in a rocking chair on her own porch. He did not ever remember seeing her flustered.

'What did you mean when you said you needed help with your mission?' he asked. 'What mission?'

'Haven't you worked it out yet, Marshal McLure?' asked the girl coolly. 'I'm a Confederate agent!'

SIXTEEN

They had left the shelter of the trees far behind them and were approaching Slaughter City across the plain. Throughout the long journey McLure had kept a wary eye open for Glanville but the town boss was nowhere to be seen on the great flat land of the high plains. They had even spent the night in an aspen grove, so that they could enter Slautara early the next morning.

'You want to ride what you told me yesterday past me again?' asked McLure, glancing at the young woman sitting imperturbably at his side. He had been thinking hard about what she had said for sometimes ever since they had broken camp. 'How can you be working for the South? You're a woman, not a spy.'

'We prefer the term scouts,' replied the girl

primly. 'Who better to move freely behind the lines? There are a few of us. Belle Boyd carried intelligence through the Union lines over twenty times before she was caught. And there are others. We convey messages, take notice of what is happening and report back to Richmond. That is how I started, after my husband was cut down. Presumably I did a good enough job because then I was sent to Slautara.'

'What were you supposed to do there?' asked McLure.

'The same as I did everywhere else,' Nora replied calmly. 'I made notes of what was happening there and reported back to my superiors. The Confederacy managed to smuggle one or two male scouts into the town, and they carried my messages back when they could. I got into the town because there is always need for nurses. And I soon found myself ... protection.'

'By living with Pete Duvall?' asked McLure, scandalized in spite of himself.

Nora flushed. 'When my husband died,'

she said with a deadly intensity, 'I vowed that I would do everything in my power to avenge his death. If that meant sleeping with Duvall to ensure my acceptance in Slaughter City, so be it.'

'All right,' said McLure swallowing hard. 'But why were you sent to Slautara. What interest did the Confederates have in the place?'

'They knew that things were not going well for the South,' said Nora. 'They needed all the edges they could get. Slaughter City was a tinder-box, especially after Glanville had blown up the Union cavalry when it attacked. My superiors thought that perhaps the unrest in the town could be utilized again to harm the Union. I was sent there to discover how the town was run and how it might be used in our cause. Glanville is the man who runs Slautara.'

'Not for much longer,' McLure told her grimly. 'He'll do his damnedest to get the money back from us and then he'll light out with it.'

'You don't seem to me to be the sort of man who would hand anything back to Glanville without a fight,' Nora told him.

'Maybe not.'

'Do you think he'll have a reception ready for us?'

McLure shook his head. He had been thinking about this too.

'No,' he answered. 'He won't risk anyone else finding the money and having to share it with them. He'll be waiting for us in Slautara with some damned plan or other.'

'He's a sharp one,' agreed the young woman. 'The cowpoke who rode into Slautara a couple of days ago, supposed to bring news of Wiley, really told Glanville that the peace had been signed. That was why Glanville moved when he did. That was the biggest payroll the fort had ever had. They were paying off most of the Union troops so that they could go home. I heard Wiley and Kearns talking about it while they waited for you.'

The young woman hesitated before she

spoke again. 'Now that you know about me, are you going to tell me what *you* were doing in Slaughter City.'

'Just another stage-coach robber on the run,' lied McLure uncomfortably.

The girl shook her head. 'You're no thief,' she said firmly. 'You came to Slautara for a purpose. And that included killing Glanville.'

'What makes you say that?' asked a jolted McLure.

'I've kept alive as a scout by using my eyes,' Nora replied. 'As soon as you became marshal it was obvious that you were an honest man. You wouldn't take bribes and you stopped the deputies accepting them too. Then when you helped Glanville rob the train today, you were as sick as a dog when you heard that the war was over, so it was no guerilla operation. And you wouldn't shoot down those Union prisoners, just because they had their hands up. You're as straight as they come, Greg. You were in Slautara like me – for reasons of your own.'

'And what makes you think I wanted to

kill Glanville?' asked McLure, trying to hide his dismay that he had been discovered so easily.

'That night when I came out of the livery stable unexpectedly, you were crouching like you were going to call on Glanville to draw. That's another reason I knew you were honest. You had plenty of chances to shoot him in the back, and you didn't take them. Well, what were you doing in Slautara?'

McLure hesitated and then told the girl of his meeting with Pinkerton and his determination to find and kill Glanville and to destroy Slaughter City. Nora heard him out and then thought carefully before she spoke.

'They chose the wrong man for the job,' she said finally. 'A spy – a scout – has to be a devious back-shooter if the need arises. You couldn't be that.'

'Maybe not,' admitted McLure, 'but I still aim to find Glanville and destroy Slaughter City. With me it's personal. Glanville betrayed my men in battle and Slautara is giving refuge to him and a whole lot of other deserters. Somehow I'm going to bring them both down. And I'm going to do it for the South, if there is a South any more. I don't want any help from the Union troops.' He looked across at the girl. 'What about you? Your work is finished now. The war is over. Will you go back to Richmond?'

Nora shook her head fiercely. 'My work will never be over,' she said seriously. 'The North killed my husband. I'll spend the rest of my life avenging his death in any way I can. The soldiers may have laid down their arms, but I can carry on fighting on my own. I'll find a way.'

McLure opened his mouth to argue with her, but one look at the girl's erect carriage and tightly clenched fists told him that it would be useless.

'You're going to ride a lonely trail,' he told her gently.

'It's my trail, Marshal McLure. And I can start by helping you when we reach Slautara.' She raised her voice to quell McLure's objections. 'I want to see a traitor like Glanville killed just as much as you do. And Slautara deserves to die as well for harbouring him and his kind.'

'All right,' said McLure. 'I'll take your help and be grateful. But you take care, you hear?'

'Stop the wagon, I'd better tend to Kearns,' was all that the girl would say.

McLure followed Nora into the back of the covered wagon, to the deputy lying among the payroll boxes. His chest was no longer bleeding but he was muttering incoherently Nora put a hand on his brow. 'He's burning up,' she said in a small voice. 'He looks dreadful. Help me change his bandages.'

As he assisted the girl in her task, McLure wondered why her reference to the wounded deputy's temperature kept echoing in his mind. Then he remembered the jeering words of Captain Jerome, the fat medical officer at Hartson Prison when McLure had tried to escape. *If you've got a fever you can convince people you've got about anything.*

McLure must have exclaimed out loud, because Nora looked at him curiously.

'What's the matter?' she asked.

'Let's put a clean shirt on Kearns when you've finished bandaging him,' Mclure said. 'Listen to me carefully I've thought of a way to bring down Slaughter City.'

SEVENTEEN

When they entered Slaughter City shortly before ten o'clock, McLure stopped off at the farrier's and bought a bucket of bubbling black pitch used for waterproofing roofs. He placed the bucket in the back of the wagon and thrust into its contents half-a-dozen thick branches he had picked up earlier in an aspen grove.

A little later he pulled up the wagon outside Doc Bernes' house. The streets of Slautara were as crowded as ever but McLure could see that there was less order, more jostling and quarrelling than he had ever seen before. There were very few deputies about either and those who were present were making few efforts to quell the disturbances.

Nora got down from the box and knocked

on the front door. After a few moments Doc Bernes opened it. He was a short, skinny, untidy man, like a bedraggled rooster. As usual he was drunk.

'Nora,' he said vaguely, swaying monotonously backwards and forwards. 'Where the hell have you been?'

'It would take too long to tell you, Doc,' said the young woman, edging past him into the house. 'Right now I need the stretcher. We've got a patient for you.'

She emerged with the canvas and wood carrier. Doc Bernes helped them lower Kearns over the tailgate and carry him into the surgery, laying him on the bed there. No traces of blood had seeped through the wounded man's shirt front.

'What's wrong with him?' asked Bernes without much interest.

'His symptoms are a high fever and spots on his chest and stomach,' Nora told him briskly, reciting the formula she had worked out with McLure on the way in. 'He's real bad, Doc.'

For a moment McLure thought that the doctor was too drunk to take in what he had been told, but there were still some remnants of medical knowledge left in the man's booze-sodden brain. Bernes's eyes widened. Involuntarily, he stepped back from the bedside.

'Do you know what you're telling me?' he howled in dismay. 'Those are the symptoms of typhoid! You've brought the disease into the town!'

'Couldn't hardly leave him to die,' said Nora innocently. 'We thought we'd better bring him straight to you.'

'Get him out of here!' screamed Bernes, jolted back into a semblance of sobriety. 'He could kill off the entire population!'

'Sorry, Doc,' said McLure, trying to look concerned. 'Kearns is one of my deputies. No way I could abandon him. You'll just have to do your best to cure him.'

'I said take him away!' shouted Bernes, white with fear. 'It may already be too late! It's the most contagious deadly disease in the West!'

McLure cupped his hand meaningfully above his holster. 'Kearns stays,' he said.

Bernes' eyes switched from the fever-ridden Kearns on the bed to the threatening McLure. He swallowed hard and turned and ran out of the house. They could hear his footsteps disappearing down the street.

'So far so good,' said Nora. 'What gave you the idea of letting the doc think it was typhoid?'

'I saw what it did to my men at Hartson prison,' McLure told her. 'Ever since the 1816 epidemic nobody in his right mind would ever stay where there was a suspected case. I've seen bigger settlements than Slautara abandoned overnight when the news got around. Typhoid frightens people more than an Apache raid.'

'With reason,' said Nora with a shudder. 'I've seen it at work as well. What happens next.'

'With any luck Doc Bernes will be spreading the word,' said McLure. 'Reckon we'll be getting a parcel of deputies along to see us before long.'

They came truculently fifteen minutes later. In that time McLure fed and watered the mules and his horse on the leadrope. He also brought in a Henry repeater and three boxes of shells.

There were four deputies in the group, pale, apprehensive-looking men who would not meet the marshal's gaze when he opened the door to their knock.

'What can I do for you boys?' asked McLure, cradling the repeater in his arms.

'Hell, Greg, is it true what the doc is saying?' asked one of them anxiously, scuffing his boot like a child before a feared teacher. 'He says Kearns has got typhoid and that you've brought him back into Slautara.'

'I'm afraid so,' McLure told him gravely. 'Doc Bernes and Nora both say there's no doubt about it. It's typhoid all right.'

'Then why have you brought him here?' demanded the scandalized deputy. 'You know what it will do to us.'

'But he's one of us,' protested McLure, wide-eyed. 'Kearns is a deputy. Surely you want me to look after him the same way I'd look after you.'

'Not if he's got typhoid!' cried a second man. 'Get him back out of town pronto!'

'Sorry, boys,' said McLure self-righteously, lifting his voice to overcome the chorus of resentful and apprehensive protests and toting his Henry an inch higher. 'I look after my men. You're welcome to come in and see Kearns for yourselves if you like.'

The four terrified men were already backing away from the door. 'You're mad, McLure,' spat one of them as they turned and scattered. 'I ain't staying here to die.'

'If you don't like it here, get out of town,' called the marshal. McLure watched the four men run like beaten dogs down the street. Then he came back into the house. Nora was looking approvingly at him. 'What do we do next?' she asked.

'We wait a while,' said McLure.

'I suppose you know that while we sit here we could get a lynch mob at the door,' she said calmly. 'Or Glanville could come looking for us to get the payroll back. What have you got to say to that, Greg McLure?'

'I'd say, ma'am, that you purely know how to reassure a man,' answered McLure.

EIGHTEEN

By the evening the carts and wagons were rolling out of town in an ever-increasing stream as the terrified inhabitants of Slautara headed away from what they thought would be a killing epidemic. The word had spread from one end of the town to the other. Frightened men and women had piled as many of their goods as they could on to any vehicles they could find and were heading desperately for the shelter of the plain. Individual horsemen mingled with the vehicles, their riders thrashing their horses to get them clear of the mass.

McLure watched the motley procession from the window of the house. He had no sympathy for the smug, well-fed citizens who had been content to benefit for so long from the presence of the outlaws and renegades in their town. The fact that they were fleeing and leaving so much behind them meant nothing to him at all. As for the deserters and gunmen going with them, they deserved everything that happened to them once they had left the shelter of Slaughter City.

One or two of the departing inhabitants shouted abuse at the doctor's house as they passed, and one even hurled a rock through a side window, shattering the glass, but when McLure emerged with his rifle at the ready even the most agitated and hate-filled among the crowd moved on hurriedly. Most of the evacuees took great care to keep right away from the home in which the deputy was said to be dying from the most deadly and dreaded of diseases.

'I never thought it would work,' marvelled Nora, standing at McLure's side and watching the massed retreat.

'Wouldn't have stayed myself if it really had been typhoid,' said McLure. ''Specially if I saw the town doctor high-tailing it for the long grass.'

'It was lucky that Bernes was drunk and a coward,' commented Nora.

'And incompetent,' said McLure. 'Don't forget incompetent.'

'I'll see how Kearns is,' said Nora.

She had been gone only a few minutes when McLure heard her call his name. He joined her in the surgery Nora was drawing the sheet over the deputy's face.

'He's dead,' she said quietly.

McLure consulted his watch. 'Time we were moving,' he said. Kearns and Wiley had both intended to kill him but he was still saddened by the death of the two men. Nora seemed to guess his thoughts. She squeezed his arm gently.

They left the doctor's house. On their way out Nora collected as many of Doc Bernes' implements and medications as she could find and stored them in her carpet bag. McLure climbed into the back of the wagon. He wrapped cloths and towels he had brought from the house around the pitch-soaked branches he had earlier placed in the bucket, and laid the branches on the floor of the wagon. Then he selected a crowbar from the collection of tools in a corner and jemmied open one of the payroll boxes. He took a wad of notes and stuffed it into his shirt pocket. He took another pile of the money and handed the notes to Nora as he joined her on the box.

'It's Yankee money,' he said. 'But it might help you get to where you're heading next.'

Nora hesitated and then inclined her head. She put the notes in the carpet bag at her feet as McLure drove the covered wagon down the street. They were going against the stream of the traffic, but the outward-bound carts were fewer in number now. Most of the inhabitants had already scattered across the plain in front of Slautara, looking for somewhere to shelter before night fell.

McLure pulled the wagon to a halt behind the livery stable. He could see that there were no horses or mules left in the barn; they had all been claimed by their owners in their headlong flight to safety. He unhitched the team of mules and drove them away, braying indignantly, to freedom up the main street.

'What do you aim to do next?' asked the girl.

'I'm going to wait for Glanville,' McLure told her. 'And while I'm waiting I'm going to burn the town down. How about you?'

'I'll wait and see you raise Cain,' said Nora. 'Then I'll head into Yankee territory and do as much harm there as I can.'

McLure picked up the first of the pitch-soaked torches and struck a match against it. He hurled the blazing branch into the straw-filled livery stable, sending the barn up in an explosion of flames and smoke. He continued up both sides of the now deserted main street, selecting every third or fourth store or saloon, smashing windows and kicking in doors to accommodate the burning deposits. Within minutes the street was ablaze, flames screaming into the sky. The fire leapt with determined agility from one untended wooden building to another, reducing each to a tortured heap of burning timber. The heat was so intense that it drove him to the centre of the street.

By the time McLure had returned to Nora, the fire was consuming the buildings in a great inferno. The town was not yet entirely deserted. Fifty yards up the street, heavily muffled against the heat, a handful of men was forming a chain to pass buckets of water from a pond behind the stores and hurl their contents on to the flames. Plainly there were still a few merchants prepared to face both typhoid and the threat of incineration in a vain attempt to save their businesses. Calmly McLure took his saddle roll and a few other effects from the back of the wagon and transferred them to his restless horse, untying her from the tailgate and leading her to safety away from the noise and glare.

'Anything you want from the wagon, better take it now,' he told Nora.

Wonderingly, the girl did as she was told,

piling a few things at her feet next to her carpet bag.

'What about Glanville?' she shouted above the din of the conflagration. 'We don't know where he is!'

'He's where he's been ever since we got back to Slautara,' said McLure. 'He's watching the payroll waiting for a chance to get at it. He's been planning that for years. Well, now he's only got one shot left at it. And he'll have to show himself to me in order to make it work.'

He took a blazing chunk of wood from the crumbling wall of the livery stable, at the same time holding it to the canvas side of the wagon. The material smouldered and then slowly tongues of fire began to creep across it.

One of the firefighters trying to contain the blaze further up the street peeled off from the group and began running frantically towards the wagon, ignoring the shouted complaints of his abandoned companions. McLure drifted towards the centre of the street and waited. As he ran, the approaching man tore the protective cloth from his face. It was Glanville.

'Damn you, McLure!' he screamed. 'What do you think you're doing? There's a fortune in that wagon. All we could ever need.'

'All *you* could need,' said McLure. 'I got other ambitions. I thought the sight of the money going up in smoke would make you break cover. Clever idea disguising yourself as a firefighter, though. I suppose you were going to work your way closer to me and then let off a snap shot. Then you saw the money-wagon on fire and you didn't have no choice but to come running.'

'Why?' demanded Glanville wildly, coming to a halt, the sweat coursing down his face. 'What did I ever do to you?'

'You rode away at Vicksburg and let the Yankees get through to my company from the flank,' said McLure. 'A lot of good men died because of you, Glanville.'

'Is that all?' croaked Glanville incredulously. 'You'd spoil the sweetest deal for that?' The town boss controlled himself and walked towards McLure. 'There's still time,' he said placatingly. 'You and me we–'

His hand sped for his gun. McLure had been waiting. McLure had been waiting ever since Vicksburg. He drove his hand down and dropped it over the handle of his Colt, bringing it up again in the same motion and firing twice. Both bullets caught Glanville square on. The town boss only managed to get off one shot and that while he was beginning to fall forward. The bullet merely sent up a cloud of dust from the street ahead of McLure. Then Glanville fell forward on to his face and lay still. McLure walked forward and knelt by Glanville's side, turning the other man on to his back. There were two bullet holes in his chest. Blood was seeping out. Glanville opened his eyes and tried to focus them on McLure.

'The sweetest deal...' he sighed, and died.

McLure walked down a side street. As he had expected, Glanville's horse, saddled and provisioned, with bulging saddle-bags, stood hitched to a post. He led the mount back to Nora, past the flames. Frightened by the shots and realizing the futility of their efforts, the amateur firefighters had given up their efforts to put out the flames and had vanished. McLure knew that in order to complete his mission he should take the torches to the residential area of the town. He no longer had any desire to do so. With Glanville dead and the business heart of Slaughter City destroyed he had no need to wreak further havoc on the town.

'She should carry you a fair distance,' he said, handing the reins of Glanville's mount to the girl. He looked round for a bucket to put out the fire in the burning wagon. It had not yet properly caught hold and he could soon bring it under control.

'Thanks,' said Nora, as McLure helped her up into the saddle.

'Which way will you go?' he asked, wanting to prolong the moment.

'North, I reckon. There's more Yankees to hoorah there.'

McLure hesitated, choosing his words with care. He realized how deep his feelings for the steadfast but driven young woman had grown over the past few days.

'You could stay with me,' he offered awkwardly, hoping that she would know what he meant, even if he could not put it into words. 'We'd make quite a team.'

Nora shook her head with certainty. 'It wouldn't work, Greg,' she said softly. 'You're more man than I've ever met, excepting maybe my husband Bill. But my hurt's too deep and I've still got too much hate left in me. I'm not like you, Greg. You've done your job. You've killed Glanville and you've destroyed the heart of the town. That was what you came to do. You can go about rebuilding your life now. You showed you'd burnt out your hatred when you spared the rest of the town just then. I can't. Not yet.' She tossed her head fiercely. 'I'm going to go North and I'm going to cause as much hurt and damnation to the Yankees I meet as I can, peace or no peace.'

'How will you live?' asked McLure.

Nora lifted her saddle-bag. 'There's always a need for a nurse,' she said. 'Especially one as well-equipped as I am now, thanks to Doc Bernes. And there's that slice of Union money you gave me. That will take me a far way until I get settled somewhere.'

'I see,' said McLure, an ache in his heart. 'Well, I guess I can only wish you luck, Nora.'

'There's one more thing you could do,' said the girl.

'What's that?'

Nora nodded at the wagon containing the payroll boxes. 'You can destroy that,' she said. She raised a hand to forestall his protests. 'I know, I know,' she said. 'You want to hand it over to Pinkerton and his men when they arrive. That would put you in mighty good standing with them. Probably get you a top job with Pinkerton in Washington.' She paused. 'Or, on the other hand, you could strike one last blow from the South. Let the fire take hold. Destroy the payroll. 'Course that would mean it would leave you wanted by Pinkerton and not much more than a saddle-tramp for a time. It's your decision, Greg.'

McLure thought about the girl's words. She sat quietly looking down at him. There was a lot in what she said. He felt oddly at peace with himself. He had achieved his aims. Glanville was dead, and with the business-centre destroyed Slaughter City would soon be no more. He owed Pinkerton nothing. He could wait for the Union troops to arrive and tell them what he had done and hand over the money almost intact. But he was still a Southerner, whatever that meant now in the new order of things. He owed nothing to the Union, not yet at any rate.

McLure made up his mind. The wagon was burning freely now. He ignored it and walked over to the smiling Nora's horse, slapping it fiercely on the rump, sending rider and mount skittering away down the street. McLure watched the girl go, aware that she was taking a sizeable chunk of his heart with her. He turned away from the blazing payroll wagon and the rest of the town. He swung into his saddle and rode slowly away in the opposite direction to the one taken by Nora.

'Let it burn,' he said, half to himself.

The publishers hope that this book has given you enjoyable reading. Large Print Books are especially designed to be as easy to see and hold as possible. If you wish a complete list of our books please ask at your local library or write directly to:

Dales Large Print Books
Magna House, Long Preston,
Skipton, North Yorkshire.
BD23 4ND

This Large Print Book, for people
who cannot read normal print,
is published under the auspices of
THE ULVERSCROFT FOUNDATION